GUILTY PARTY

A forensic physician seeks answers after two lawyers are murdered

CANDY DENMAN

THE BOOK FOLKS

Paperback edition published by

The Book Folks

London, 2020

ISBN 978-1-913516-34-5

www.thebookfolks.com

GUILTY PARTY is the third book in a series of medical crime fiction titles featuring police doctor Callie Hughes. Look out for the first and second books, DEAD PRETTY and BODY HEAT, and the fourth, fifth, and sixth, VITAL SIGNS, DEADLY REMEDIES, and MURDER LUST, available on Kindle and in paperback.

Prologue

He stops to adjust the strap of the leather harness that is cutting into his shoulder and distracting him from his pleasure. Finally satisfied that everything is perfect, he hangs suspended from a hook on the back of the solid wood door, with a studded belt around his neck. The belt is cutting in and reducing the flow of oxygen to his brain, not completely, but enough to enhance the length and depth of an orgasm. He has the segment of orange in his mouth, gripped between his teeth, already primed with amyl nitrite, ready for when he climaxes. He is close now.

As his orgasm reaches its peak, he leans forward to tighten the belt around his neck, cutting off the blood supply to his brain even more, and then bites down on the orange segment, breathing in the precious fumes. He writhes in ecstasy as his hand reaches up to the release clip on the harness, just aware enough to know he needs to free himself the moment the orgasm ends. At last it begins to subside. He is on the verge of losing consciousness as his fingers close around the clasp, pressing the release button. It doesn't open. He panics, struggles to stand, trying to release the pressure on his neck, but his legs have gone soft, they no longer have the power to raise his body and take the weight off the belt around his neck. He tries one more time, fingers scrabbling at the unresponsive clip, body jerking with the effort of trying to stand up, before he gives up and slumps, defeated, fading into unconsciousness as nature take its course, and his life.

Chapter 1

Over the buzz of her electric toothbrush, Callie heard the strains of Mozart's 40th symphony and realised that her mobile must be ringing somewhere in the flat. She hurriedly spat in the basin, grabbed a hand towel and went into the living room, wiping her mouth as she ran.

"Dr Hughes speaking," she said as soon as she had caught her breath. Clamping the phone in place with her shoulder, she pulled her dressing gown more closely round her because it made her feel more professional to be, if not properly dressed, at least decent. Ready for whatever work the day brought.

"Mike Parton here, Dr Hughes. We've had a sudden death reported at 20 B, Winslow Gardens, St Leonards."

Mike Parton was the coroner's officer. An ex-policeman, who always wore a plain black suit and matching black tie, so that his clothing, as well as his demeanour, was like that of a funeral director. He was undeniably well-suited to his work.

"Any other information?" she asked and there was a slight pause. She knew Parton hated to tell her anything; that he wanted her to arrive at the location without any preconceived ideas, but Callie found it helped to be mentally prepared for whatever she was about to see. It also gave her the chance to make sure she had all the necessary equipment, like menthol rub to cover the smell of decomposition from an over-ripe corpse.

"Probable auto-erotic asphyxiation last night."

Callie grimaced, but at least the body would be fresh. In general, she was fine with the macabre and distressing details of a sudden death. It was the people left behind, shocked and unprepared for the event, that got to her. At times there would be bewilderment: Why? How? At others, intense grief, or worse, indifference, but almost always there would be some loss of dignity, for both the dead and their survivors. Sudden death usually caught people at a bad moment, but sudden death during sex, whilst many would argue that it was a good way to go, meant there was little room for dignity, particularly if it was during an unnatural or unusual sexual act, because the press would have a field day.

"I'll meet you there," she told him and ended the call before immediately going to her contacts to find the number she wanted. It was number one on her speed dial. There were only two numbers she called regularly enough to be allocated a speed dial code, her day job and her best friend Kate.

"Hi Linda, it's Callie."

"Bugger."

"Yeah, sorry. It's a sudden death. Hopefully won't be too late, but—" Callie listened to the long and heart-felt sigh coming from Linda's end of the phone. Crying off a fully booked surgery because of her other work with the police was an unfortunately all too frequent occurrence, and she knew it.

"Sorry," she said again, even though she knew it didn't help, at all.

"I'll cancel as many appointments as I can and see who I can palm the others off on." Linda sounded resigned to the inevitable. She was a good practice manager, but it was a hard job, and Callie certainly didn't make it any easier.

"Thanks, Linda, and tell Gauri I'll take some of her visits to make up for it."

Callie knew that Dr Sinha was the only one of her colleagues who would agree to take any of her patients; the others all resented being asked to help when she was called out by the coroner's office. They wanted her to give up her part-time hobby, as they saw it, and concentrate fully on her job as a real doctor, a local general practitioner, with all the responsibilities that brought with it: her patients, her colleagues, her staff. Every time she ditched them in favour of a corpse, she was letting them down – all of them – but what could she say? She loved the buzz.

* * *

When she arrived at the address Parton had given her, Callie saw that it was part of an elegant Victorian terrace. The majority of the houses in the street had long since been split into flats, and as she was looking for number 20 B, she had guessed that she was looking for one of them. She removed her jacket, intending to leave it safely in her car. She had deliberately dressed in clothing that was machine washable, but she would still try her best to keep it uncontaminated by death, or at least body fluids.

She pulled her long blonde hair back into a clip and snapped on a pair of latex gloves. Not only did she mean to get as little of the scene as possible onto herself, she wanted to prevent any transfer of herself onto the scene. She never knew when a supposedly natural death could turn out to be anything but. That was what she was there for, to make that first call on the death: natural, if unexpected, or suspicious. Once she gave her opinion that an apparently natural death might be suspicious, then the full forensic circus was wheeled out, with all its subsequent cost implications for the police, so she had to be careful – careful not to instigate full investigations for too many innocent and natural deaths but equally careful not to miss any possible murders or manslaughters.

Dr Calliope Harriet Hughes MBChB MRCGP DipFMS, part-time local general practitioner and part-time forensic physician for the Hastings police. Dr Hughes to her patients, and Callie to her friends. Tall and slim, elegant, in an understated, natural way; her straight, shoulder-length, blond hair kept neatly away from her face with a clip. Cool, precise, well-ordered, in looks and in life. With just a hint of fire, a slight glint in her eye, a slight twitch at the corner of her mouth that let you know there was a lot more going on than she was prepared to let out from under that steely exterior.

At number 20, she rang the bell marked B and noted that the house appeared to have been split into only three flats, whereas some she had passed had five or six bells next to the front door. She was let into the front hall by a young constable she didn't recognise. Then a woman who looked to be in her late thirties, overweight and dressed in the sort of clothes that were made for comfort rather than looks, appeared out from the ground floor flat holding a mug of tea and a plate of chocolate biscuits. The constable hesitated and Callie realised that he was uncertain whether he should accept them in front of her.

"Don't mind me. It could be a long morning."

He gratefully took the tea and a couple of the biscuits, nodding his thanks to the woman as he shoved in most of a hobnob.

"Can I get you something?" the woman asked Callie, who politely declined.

"I'd better go on up." Callie looked questioningly at the constable.

"It's on the first floor." He indicated the stairs, trying not to choke on the biscuit, but clearly not intending to follow her up. "They're expecting you. I'd better stay with the lady who found the body," he explained, glancing into the ground floor flat where Callie could see a tearful young woman clasping a mug to her chest as the older woman fussed around her.

Callie was glad the constable was staying in the hall, even if it was only because the young woman was pretty and distressed. At least she wouldn't have too big an audience inside the flat, and it was only as she mounted the stairs that she wondered whom he was referring to when he said 'they'.

At the top of the stairs, the large and solid door from the hallway was open and she went into the drawing room. It was always good to get the feel of a place before examining the body. The room was high-ceilinged and elegant, in both the architecture and furnishing style. Her gaze moved round, taking in the original but uninspired artwork on the walls, the heavy brocade curtains, and Mike Parton, standing by a second doorway talking to Detective Inspector Steve Miller. Callie hesitated as she felt a sudden lurch in her stomach. Whatever else, she hadn't expected to see Miller here, and wherever Miller was...

"Looks like one of them rubber chickens you see in joke shops." Detective Sergeant Bob Jeffries came through the doorway, older than his boss, with his ginger hair now grey, Jeffries had no time for political correctness or diplomacy and knew that he would never be promoted as a result. "Proper trussed up like one and all, boss. Oh, hello, Dr Hughes," he said with a grin as he noticed Callie. "Prepare yourself, the pervert's not a pretty sight."

Miller and Parton both turned to look at her and Callie could feel the burning sensation rising up from her chest, the hot flush of red climbing up her neck and, yes, finally reaching her cheeks.

"What are you two doing here?" she asked, rather too curtly, in an attempt to hide her embarrassment.

"What's the matter, Doc? Aren't you pleased to see us?" Jeffries asked.

"I'm sorry, Dr Hughes," Parton quickly cut in, coming towards her, "but once the location was out, this was bound to happen."

"He's known to the police then?" She directed her question to him, rather than either of the two detectives.

"Oh, yes. He's well-known to us," Miller replied and she turned to look at him. He was just as handsome as she remembered: the slight bend in his nose, the result of an ancient rugby injury; the feathery lines around each eye, irises a deep, rich hazel with a touch of amber; the slight dimple at each side of his mouth. She took a deep breath.

"This isn't the sort of place I'd expect an old lag to live." She gestured at the opulent room.

"No, but it's exactly the sort of place you'd expect a lying bastard criminal defence lawyer to own." It was Jeffries who answered her, inevitably. "I had to come and check he was really dead."

* * *

In the bedroom, Callie approached the body. It was hanging by the neck from a short chain attached to a solid-looking hook on the back of the door that lead into the bathroom. She tried to hide her disgust as she checked the dead man for a radial pulse. She couldn't get to the carotids because of what looked like a studded leather dog collar around his neck and attached to his bondage harness.

There was no pulse and she let his arm drop, accidentally setting the body into motion. It was hard to ignore the slight wave of his genitalia hanging flaccidly from the open crotch of his tight PVC shorts as the body swayed, or the smell of body fluids released at the moment of death that wafted from them. She was just glad that it wasn't her job to undress him for the post-mortem. She took out her stethoscope and found a place between the straps and paraphernalia where she could listen to his chest whilst steadying his body with her other hand. She could hear no heartbeat or breath sounds.

"Death confirmed," she said quietly. Parton took out his notebook, writing down the time death was pronounced and who by, for the record.

"I think I could've told you that," Jeffries said as Parton gave him a reproving look, but there was no stopping Jeffries' mouth, as Callie knew only too well.

She stepped back, away from the smell, and looked at the body in situ. It was hard to see his face under the rubber mask, but judging by the greying hair and the incipient paunch hanging over the waistband of his shorts, he was a well-nourished, middle-aged man. His home was spacious and expensively furnished, situated in by no means the cheap end of town. What made an obviously successful and otherwise intelligent man do stuff like this? Callie asked herself. She couldn't even begin to imagine the answer.

As soon as she had pronounced death and stepped back, the photographer had gone back to work, taking pictures not only of the body, but also of a segment of an orange, slightly chewed, that was lying on the floor just below him.

"How come you got the happy snapper out when it's not a suspicious death?" Jeffries asked Parton.

"I wanted to be sure we had all the angles covered," Mike replied, looking ever so slightly sheepish.

"Don't tell me you're pandering to the middle-class tendency to sue, Mike." Miller couldn't help a small smile.

"Well, he is, was, a solicitor, so litigation is always a possibility should any of his family or colleagues be unhappy with our findings."

"Glad it's not just to pass the photos round amongst your mates when you're out for the weekly beer and curry night." Jeffries laughed and Parton winced. He was the least likely person to indulge in a beer and curry night, or to allow the pictures to be shown round, either. Callie was quite sure the pictures would only go as far as the coroner and then be safely locked away. Not deigning to reply to Jeffries, Parton pointed to an open ampoule on the table. Callie went over and looked at it.

"Amyl nitrite."

"That's a popper, isn't it? To prolong orgasm?" Miller asked and Callie nodded as she carefully put the ampoule into an evidence bag.

"He probably emptied it onto the orange segment on the floor there, which he then put in his mouth so that he could bite on it when he was close to–"

"Yeah," Jeffries interjected, "I'm guessing he would have had his hands too full to break it at that point."

No one felt the need to add anything to that.

Once the photographer had finished, Callie picked up the bitten orange segment with her gloved hands, placed it carefully in another evidence bag and instructed Mike Parton to keep it, and all the equipment around and attached to the body, as evidence, just in case. He was also not to remove any of the clothing or harness until the coroner had seen it, even though she knew he would do that anyway. It was normal protocol in a case of sudden death such as this, whether or not there were any suspicious circumstances. The body would be transported to the morgue looking every bit as stupid as when he was found. He was to be spared no indignities.

"It's a natural death as far as you're concerned then?" Miller checked with her.

"Natural? You've got to be joking, guv. There's nothing natural about dressing up in rubber and letting your John Thomas dangle like that."

Whilst Callie might agree in part with Jeffries' views, she wasn't going to give him the satisfaction of knowing it.

"I don't think we're looking at a suspicious death, no," Callie said and turned away.

In fact, it was as clear a case of auto-erotic asphyxiation as she was ever likely to see, but the coroner was known to be particular about no one interfering with the evidence before he saw it, no matter how cut and dried a case it was likely to be.

With that, she left the bedroom and escaped back into the drawing room, followed by Parton carrying a box of evidence bags.

"Can you just countersign, Dr Hughes?" Parton asked her and she went over to the table where he was putting it down. Callie was kept busy putting her initials on the seals and labels on the evidence bags and signing the log, and barely acknowledged Miller's goodbye as he and Jeffries left, satisfied that the solicitor was, indeed, dead. No doubt his manner of death would be the subject of crude jokes in the station canteen for months to come.

"Are we done?" Callie asked Parton when the last bag had been replaced in the box, duly signed and labelled. "Only I really ought to get back to surgery."

Meticulous as ever, Parton checked his list and counted the bags one last time.

"What the bloody hell's going on here?" A woman's voice, sharp and haughty, someone who was used to getting her own way, came from the hallway. There was the sound of a much more squeaky reply, presumably from the poor girl who had found the body.

"For goodness' sake, pull yourself together and tell me what's going on," the voice continued, but was followed by a deeper, more soothing voice as Parton strode towards the open flat door to find out who was there.

"Give the girl a chance, Antonia."

"Excuse me, madam—"

The constable belatedly tried to intervene, but footsteps were rapidly coming up the stairs and two people came into the room before Parton or the constable had the chance to stop them. A man and a woman. He was in his early forties, hair kept a little on the long side, flecks of grey at the temple, well manicured, immaculately dressed in a conservative grey suit and tie; he looked every inch the provincial solicitor. She was in her thirties, her dark brown hair well cut in a sharp, angular style, but her pin-striped suit was made slightly less severe and business like by her scarlet nail varnish, not to mention the fishnet tights and four-inch spike heels she was wearing.

Parton held up his hand to stop them coming any further into the room. The crime scene investigators had not yet finished and the body had not yet been removed. It was Parton's job to keep everything uncontaminated until the scene was declared clear. Once he was satisfied that the body had been removed and nothing else needed to be done, and not until then, would he allow anyone else in, and then, only the next of kin or whoever they requested be allowed entry.

"Please, just stay where you are," he said firmly.

"Who are you?" the woman, Antonia, Callie presumed, asked him.

"Coroner's officer. Mike Parton. And you are?"

"Antonia Hersham." She held out her hand and Mike automatically shook it. "And this is my colleague and partner at Townsend and Bartlett, Mervyn Bartlett."

Mike shook his hand as well, before the rather daunting Antonia turned her attentions to Callie.

"Dr Hughes, forensic physician." She introduced herself quickly, but Antonia was clearly unimpressed and turned her attention back to Parton.

"I take it something has happened to Giles Townsend? I mean, I can't imagine he'd need a coroner's officer unless he was dead."

Callie looked at Parton. He didn't look happy.

"I'm sure you understand that we would prefer to say nothing until we have a formal identification and the family have been informed," he told her firmly. "Now, if you wouldn't mind?" He tried to usher them back towards the door.

"Mervyn can identify him for you, can't you, Mervyn?" She stood her ground, and gestured for Mervyn to come forward, but he didn't look so sure that he wanted to.

"No!" Parton said a little too quickly as if he thought the poor man would suddenly charge into the bedroom and see his partner strung up on the back of the door.

Mervyn looked relieved.

"It will have to wait until we have transported the body back to the mortuary. It's often best if the next of kin identify the body, but if that is not possible, I will contact you." Parton recovered his control of the situation.

Antonia turned to Callie.

"What was it? His heart? Or did he have a stroke? I always said he was too stressed for his own good."

"I couldn't possibly say until after the post-mortem." Callie tactfully put her off, even though she had a pretty good idea about the cause of death. "Perhaps you could give us the name and address of his next of kin?"

"Of course. His wife Harriet. I'll write down her address and telephone number for you." Mervyn looked very pleased to have something practical and not too grim that he could do.

"She doesn't live here, then?"

"God, no, they have a large house in Hawkhurst, this was just Giles's pied-à-terre." Mervyn wrote the details down and handed them to Callie with a little smile. Callie handed the piece of paper on to Parton. It was him who would have the task of breaking the news to Mrs Townsend and getting her to identify her husband, but not until after all the bondage gear had been removed, she hoped.

"Well, if there's nothing we can do here?" Antonia seemed reluctant to go, but her partner was moving towards the door.

"I think we should get poor Penny back to the office and get her a nice strong cup of tea," Mervyn said and then added, for Callie and Mike's benefit, "Penny's our receptionist. We sent her over here to find out what had happened when Giles didn't show up for a breakfast meeting and didn't answer his phone. She found the body, poor lass. Been a terrible shock."

"I can imagine." Callie was sure poor Penny would be telling everyone in the office all about exactly how she found the body for weeks to come. It would certainly take her that long before she could erase the image from her mind, if she ever did manage to do that.

"She had a key?"

A look of anxiety passed across Mervyn's face but Antonia didn't even blink.

"Giles sometimes worked here and Penny would come and collect paperwork. I'd better just check his desk–"

Antonia moved towards the desk by the window but was headed off by Mike Parton.

"I'm sorry, Ms Hersham, but I must insist you do not touch anything. Not until you have permission from the next of kin."

"But–"

"Penny," Mervyn reminded her. "We need to get her back."

"Yes, of course." At last Antonia seemed to realise that she had no hope of getting past Parton and Callie and resigned herself to the disappointment. "Right, yes, let's get Penny back and give her a chance to talk it through. Get it off her chest." She nodded at Callie and Mike and left, with Mervyn in tow, as two mortuary attendants arrived with a stretcher to transport the body.

"Get all the gory details, more like," Callie said to Parton.

He nodded agreement.

"I'd best be off too, if you've finished with me?"

"I don't suppose I could prevail upon you to come with me to break the news to the widow, could I?"

Callie must have looked unenthusiastic, so he continued, "I know it's a liberty and you're a very busy woman, but we've nearly finished here and it's not going to be easy, explaining it to her, how it happened, I mean." Callie realised that Parton, so good at breaking bad news to loved ones and relatives, was uncomfortable with the sexual aspect of this death. Even more uncomfortable than she was.

"Mike, I think that's probably the understatement of the year." With a sigh, Callie agreed to go with him. "Might as well be hung for a sheep as a lamb, but I need to be back in time to do some visits."

Chapter 2

The house in Hawkhurst turned out to be a substantial neo-gothic pile about a mile outside the village and, being set in dense woodland, looked as if it could have been used as a set in a Hammer horror film. Callie parked her midnight blue, convertible Audi TT on the ample driveway behind Parton's more prosaic but equally immaculate Vauxhall Nova and got out. She looked at the house dubiously.

"His colleagues didn't mention children."

"No, but it is rather large for two people on their own – better be prepared."

"I still don't know how you persuaded me to come along," she grumbled as they approached the imposing front door, thinking that Giles Townsend could have fathered an entire football team and it still wouldn't have occurred to his colleagues to warn them.

"Because I'm just a wonderful human being? Or you felt sorry for me? Maybe it's because you are a soft touch." Parton smiled at her, knowing very well that it was none of these; it was because of overwhelming curiosity. She was wondering what sort of woman was married to the man who had risked his life, and lost it, in the pursuit of a longer and better climax. Parton knew her far too well.

"Whatever the reason, I will need to take a very large cake in to work to make up for this."

"Take my advice, make it yourself. A home-made cake says so much more."

Callie snorted in amusement.

"You've clearly never tasted my cooking then. I want the cake to show how much I appreciate them, not give them all food poisoning."

Parton smiled again, but she wasn't joking. Cooking, and in particular baking, had never been one of Callie's strengths.

There was an antique brass bell knob, but there was no sound when Parton tried it, so he used a knocker shaped in the likeness of a lion's head instead. They both stood still and listened for a response. At first all they could hear was the yapping of a small dog, coming from somewhere deep in the recesses of the house. Then it was joined by the deeper bark of something larger.

"Could you live in a place like this?" Callie asked as they waited.

Parton looked around him. There were no other houses in sight, just the lane disappearing through the woods.

"No problem. Nice and quiet, wouldn't get disturbed by the neighbours, that's for sure."

Callie shivered.

"I prefer to have all my basic needs in walking distance, not to mention the reassuring feeling that if I screamed for help, someone might actually hear."

"That doesn't mean to say they'd do anything about it. A scream for help would get zero response in a lot of places."

Callie had to concede that he was probably right. Maybe she should move further out, particularly as the young man currently living on the ground floor of her house almost certainly wouldn't hear her screams over the noise of the diabolical thrash metal music he played so loud that the bass beat rattled the windows.

At last they heard footsteps and a voice calling out, "Do be quiet, Tucker! Lady! In here."

There was a yelp, some scuffling and the sound of a door slamming, and then the front door opened with a rattle of chains to reveal a middle-aged woman who looked at them enquiringly.

"Yes?"

Parton stepped forward.

"Mrs Townsend?"

"And you are?"

Callie had a chance to look more closely at the woman whose husband had trussed himself up for solitary sex, and found that she looked completely and unexpectedly normal. Callie could tell that she had been pretty enough as a young woman, but now she was in her fifties and a bit on the plump side. Her hair had been allowed to turn grey naturally and fell to her shoulders in what should have been a neat, straight style, but was softened by a breakout of natural waves. Her only concessions to adornment were one small gold stud in each earlobe and a single-strand gold chain around her neck. Callie bet that the woman was a member of the Women's Institute, was on the Parish Council and had no shortage of invitations for lunch.

"Mike Parton. Coroner's officer for Hastings and St Leonards." Parton showed his ID, holding it high and steady, giving Mrs Townsend plenty of time to check it. "Could we come in for a moment?"

Mrs Townsend stepped back, allowing them to enter the spacious hall. There was continuous yapping and a disgruntled bark from behind one of the doors that led into the hall, and the sound of claws scratching against the wood.

"Quiet!" Mrs Townsend said sharply to the perpetrators, and there was a slight whine as the animals obeyed, but the continuing snuffling sound suggested that at least one of the dogs was far from happy about being kept away from the visitors.

The floor in the hall had black and white ceramic floor tiles and was furnished with large pieces of heavy, dark Jacobean-style furniture that would have looked out of place in a smaller room, but fitted the house and its atmosphere perfectly.

Mrs Townsend was leading them through into another room, and Callie's over-active imagination half expected it to be a torture chamber or a dungeon. Mr Townsend would seem to have been into that scene, so it was entirely possible his wife was some sort of dominatrix, although, Callie had to admit, she didn't look like one. His colleague, Antonia Hersham was far more what Callie imagined a dominatrix would be like than this rather mousy, grandmotherly woman. As she entered the room, Callie was surprised to find it was a pleasantly light and chintzy sitting room, with the sun pouring through the tall windows, showing up the dust motes and making them dance. It seemed to suit Mrs Townsend far more than the dark and overbearing hall.

"Do sit down," Mrs Townsend told them. "I'm going to put the kettle on, make some coffee, I take it you'll both have one?"

"Mrs Townsend–" Parton started, but she interrupted him, holding up her hand to stop him mid-sentence.

"No. I will make coffee first, Mr Parton. I suspect whatever news a coroner's officer brings, it won't be good, particularly when he brings a woman along to cope with the tears. I shall need a good strong coffee to get me through it." And she went out, leaving Parton and Callie to sit and wait.

As they heard Mrs Townsend open the door to the kitchen, there were some sudden loud yelps and the sound of claws skittering across the hall floor.

"Tucker! Lady!" Mrs Townsend called as a small black mongrel with more than a hint of Jack Russell in his ancestry came racing into the sitting room and skidded to a halt, to be almost bowled over by the larger, slower chocolate Labrador following. The terrier stood his ground, barking and yapping at the two strangers who had invaded his territory, but picking out Parton as the bigger threat, whilst the Lab jumped up, stuck two enormous paws on Callie's lap, dribbling and wagging its tail violently. She pushed the dog gently but firmly to the floor and fished in her bag for a tissue to wipe the worst of the slobber off.

"There's a good girl." Parton didn't look entirely at ease as he held his hand tentatively out to the smaller dog, snapping his fingers and making soothing noises.

Callie took a closer look at the animal.

"I think you'll find that he's a good boy, actually, Mike."

He checked the dog out as Callie picked at some of the brown hairs that had stuck to her cream jumper.

At last Mrs Townsend returned with a tray holding delicate porcelain mugs, a jug of milk, a sugar bowl, a brimming cafetiere of coffee and a plate of digestives.

"Just help yourselves, please." She sat back. "So, come along then. Tell me what's happened. It's Giles, isn't it? Is he dead?"

Parton cleared his throat and stirred his coffee vigorously, obviously hoping that Callie would jump in, but she glared at him. He was much more used to this than she was, and it was definitely in his job description to break the news of a sudden death, not hers.

"I'm very sorry to have to tell you that your husband's body was discovered at his flat in St Leonards first thing this morning."

Mrs Townsend said nothing for a moment or two and then took a sip of coffee.

"Who found him? I hope it wasn't Mrs Kanchowski, she's got a weak heart and it really would have upset her."

"Mrs Kanchowski?" Parton queried.

"The cleaner. Lovely woman, but prone to nerves," Mrs Townsend explained.

"No, it was the receptionist from his law firm. When he didn't turn up for work…' Parton petered out.

"Poor child. I hope she doesn't get nightmares about it. Where did it happen? In his bed?"

"Er, no." It seemed as if Parton intended to leave it at that.

"The bathroom, judging by your face. I'd heard that most heart attacks happen on the loo. How awful for him. He was a great one for dignity in his working life, he would have hated for her to find him with his trousers round his ankles."

Parton looked at Callie in desperation and she realised that he didn't know what to say. For a man who spent his working life informing relatives about their loved ones' last moments, he had no idea what to tell Mrs Townsend. Callie wasn't sure that she did either.

"Excuse me, Mrs Townsend. Forgive me, but although we will know more once the post-mortem is done, I think we can be pretty sure it wasn't actually a heart attack that killed your husband."

Mrs Townsend looked at Callie directly for the first time.

"Oh, I just assumed…" She hesitated for a moment, sensing that Callie and Parton were both trying to tell her something. "Come along, out with it. How exactly did he die?"

"Auto-asphyxiation." Callie came out with it, at last. "That's when—"

"Yes, yes. I'm perfectly well aware of what auto-asphyxiation means." Mrs Townsend interrupted her and looked more than a little red in the face. They sat in silence for a moment whilst the full implications of her husband's mode of death sank in.

"Oh, Lord! Everyone's going to know, aren't they?"

The Labrador chose that moment to take advantage of her owner's distraction and tried to remove a biscuit from the plate in front of her.

"Lady Markwick! Don't you dare!" Mrs Townsend said sharply and the dog sank down with an apologetic look on her face.

"Can we keep the cause of death quiet?" she continued to Parton.

"It is confidential information, of course, but there will have to be an inquest." He fiddled with his cup, anxiously. "It's the law, we have no choice."

"Will the press be there? At the inquest?"

Parton nodded.

"I think it's likely. I'm sorry."

"That's not going to be nice. He will always be remembered as the man who, who–" Her voice broke slightly as she took a deep breath and absent-mindedly fed another biscuit to the dogs. "Is there no way we can keep the details from getting out? Have a closed inquest? What do they call hearings where the press isn't allowed? In camera?"

Parton cleared his throat.

"I can ask the coroner, but–" He didn't seem to hold out much hope, but she clutched at the straw.

"Thank you, I would appreciate that." She seemed to make a decision. "I'll get his partners onto it as well. I'm sure they won't want it to get out that their colleague indulged in these, well, this type of practice."

"Did you know that he did?" Callie couldn't resist asking. "Indulge in these practices, I mean."

Mrs Townsend hesitated again and then shook her head.

"Not really. We lead separate lives, have done for years. At the beginning, we – or rather I – wanted children, but Giles wasn't so keen, had his little peccadilloes, shall we say, not that I knew the extent of them. Nothing like this, I mean. I was willing to try or do almost anything to get a child, our child, but once it became obvious that we weren't going to be having any, there didn't seem much point trying any more and he continued with his interests alone."

"But you stayed together?"

"Yes. It's not that we hated each other or anything. We just had different ways of life. Giles did what he wanted in the confines of his own flat and left me alone. He was very generous. I got the house and he'd come and stay from time to time, in his own room, of course, and I went with him to official functions and to all the social dos where a wife is needed."

Callie looked at Mrs Townsend with a complete lack of comprehension. How could anyone live a life like that? Two people, so separate, but still married. People, and the compromises they were prepared to make in life, never ceased to amaze her.

"We will need someone to make a formal identification of the body, Mrs Townsend." Parton cut in, clearly worried that Callie might just voice her thoughts.

"Of course. I'll just need to get changed, put on something more suitable."

Callie and Parton were happy to let her go and change. They knew that the bereaved often fussed about the unimportant details as a way of stopping themselves from thinking about the bigger, more distressing ones. It was a form of displacement activity, like arranging the funeral and contacting relatives. If people could only understand just how much the bereaved needed to do these small practical things in order to help them cope and come to terms with the death of a loved one, they wouldn't insist on always rushing in and taking them over. Time after time, they had both heard the recently bereaved talk about how they wished they had been allowed to sort out the funeral, contact the bank, or make their own dinner, anything to take their mind off their future, alone.

As they waited for Harriet Townsend to return, the front-door bell rang and Tucker went into a frenzy of yapping again.

"I'll see who that is," Callie called out to Mrs Townsend and went to open the front door, hanging on to Tucker's collar as she did so, whilst Parton tried to hang on to Lady Markwick, the Labrador.

Standing on the front doorstep, looking surprised to see her, were Antonia Hersham and Mervyn Bartlett.

"What are you doing here?" Antonia asked sharply.

"My job," Callie answered curtly, irritated by the lawyer's attitude. "What are you doing here?" Although she was pretty sure that Giles Townsend's partners had heard how he had died by now and were rallying round to try and prevent the details getting out.

Much to Callie's disappointment, both Mike Parton and Mervyn Bartlett stepped forward to intervene at this point.

"Mrs Townsend is just changing her clothes, she'll be down in a minute," Parton said hurriedly.

"We came to give our condolences," Mervyn said at the same time.

Callie stepped back from the door to let them in. She was just in time, as Antonia had moved forward, either confident that Callie would move, or uncaring whether she did or not and quite prepared to push her out of the way if necessary.

Mervyn followed with an apologetic smile.

Callie closed the door and let Tucker loose, pleased to see that the dog went straight for Antonia and jumped up at her, catching her fishnet tights, and pulling a hole in them.

"You are such a naughty boy, Tucker!" Mrs Townsend said as she came down the stairs to see who her visitors were, but her tone was insincere and even held the slightest hint of satisfaction at the dog's behaviour. "I'm terribly sorry, Antonia, everything is in such a muddle today."

Antonia put on her best sympathetic face, and to do her justice, it was almost convincing.

"Harriet, Harriet, don't worry about it at all." She hesitated and glanced at Mervyn. "We are so sorry about poor Giles. You must be devastated. If there's anything, absolutely anything we can do, you will tell us, won't you?" She reached out and laid her hand on Mrs Townsend's forearm, but the new widow brushed her aside.

"I have to go and identify the body now, Antonia. I'm sorry to hurry away, but you do understand, don't you? These things have to be done."

"Of course, we understand," Mervyn replied, but there was no mistaking the look of anger on Antonia's face at being summarily dismissed in public and it gave Callie great satisfaction.

Chapter 3

It was an awfully long time later, or so it seemed to Callie, that she was able to get away from the surgery, her patients and all the necessary grovelling and apologies to her colleagues, to meet up with Kate, a local solicitor, in their favourite pub, The Stag.

"Tell me all about it or I will have to forcibly extract the details from you," Kate said as she set down her pint of Spitfire and two packets of crisps, and started to remove some of her layers of clothing: a deep maroon velvet coat, purple and crimson knitted scarf, black gloves, red hat. Her dark, almost black hair, tumbled out over her midnight blue jumper as she pulled the hat off, throwing it and her other outerwear into a heap at the end of the bench next to Callie, before sitting opposite her. Kate and Callie had been friends since school, and were exact opposites. Where Callie was slim and blonde, Kate was dark and voluptuous; where Callie was cool and considered, Kate was warm and unpredictable; whilst Callie usually wore neat, tailored clothes in neutral colours, Kate wore rich jewel colours, layered in a seemingly haphazard manner. Chalk and cheese, they had been close friends and confidantes for many years.

"I take it you've heard about Giles Townsend then?" Callie said.

"It's been the talk of every law firm in town, so come on, was he really found in a dominatrix dungeon full of whips and instruments of torture?"

"No! And you know I can't talk about it. It will all come out at the inquest." Callie took a sip of her white wine spritzer and picked at a crisp. "Anyway, how come it's the talk of the town? I would have thought his colleagues would have done their best to keep it quiet."

"Oh, they are desperately trying to deny everything, especially as they were seriously positioning themselves as upmarket. You know, getting rich celebs and politicians off drink driving and wife-beating charges, usually by highlighting faults in police procedure."

"I can see why he was so popular with the police now."

"Absolutely. But you know, any publicity is good publicity, particularly if you want the business of every pervert in East Sussex, and let's face it, who wouldn't? Anything to make the law more interesting." Kate emptied the last of the salt and vinegar crisps into her hand and scrumpled the packet up before opening the next. Out of the corner of her eye, Callie watched the packet slowly unfurl again.

"They don't really seem the types, to be honest; way too straight, but then I'd probably have said the same of Mr Townsend." Unable to stop herself, Callie picked up the crisp packet and straightened it out, neatly folding it in half and anchoring it under the menu holder, to be disposed of when she next went up to the bar.

"It's always the ones you least expect." Kate was used to her friend's fastidious ways and knew better than to remark on them. "I mean, look at Doreen Ponting."

"Who?"

"Come on, Callie, keep up. She's the local Crown Prosecution Service Chief and she's been featuring in the tabloids all week."

"Why?"

Kate sighed.

"She's been done for driving under the influence and no problems with police procedure this time, let me tell you."

"She should know better." Callie had no sympathy with drink drivers, having dealt with the consequences of their actions too many times.

"Exactly. And not just that, she was found completely comatose behind the wheel of her car, parked at a well-known dogging site near Eastbourne and in a state of undress. The pictures have been all over the internet."

"How on earth did anyone get pictures?"

"Presumably someone who was at the place recognised her and realised what a scoop it was."

"Probably someone she has prosecuted in the past."

"Almost certainly."

"Talk about courting danger! Surely it must have occurred to her that she would be recognised sooner or later?"

"I know. You hear about politicians sexting teenagers and stuff like that because they get off on the possibility of being caught, but the head of the CPS?"

"Unbelievable." Callie shook her head at the stupidity of others.

"Of course, even the tabloids have been more circumspect than to actually publish the worst photos, which is why the photographer has put them on the web. Brilliant, isn't it?"

Kate finished her beer and looked at Callie's still almost full wine glass.

"Another spritzer?"

"No, look, I'll get you a pint." Callie stood up, grabbing her bag and the empty crisp packet.

"Sit down, I'll get myself one for now and you can get the next round, unless you're rushing off somewhere?"

"No, it's okay, I've no plans for tonight."

"Excellent, two old maids out on the town together. I suggest a night of beer, wine and calorie-laden food. We could even go to the Adelaide and see if we can pick up an Italian waiter each, if you like."

"No way. Last time I went to the Adelaide I only managed to pick up a schoolboy and a serial killer."

"That's not strictly true, though, is it? Because I seem to remember you also managed to bump into a certain Detective Inspector, too." Kate left Callie to her blushes and thoughts as she went to the bar for her beer.

Detective Inspector Miller. Callie had started out disliking him intensely, thinking that he was the sort of man who beat up handcuffed prisoners, that he was arrogant and a bully, but then, as she got to know him better, her opinion of him had changed. He was complex, strong, and dependable. He liked to be right, yes, but he was prepared to listen to arguments and change his mind where necessary. Oh, he was still irritating and occasionally patronising, but over the last few months, Callie had found herself more and more attracted to him. It was just a shame that he was married, and therefore out of bounds as far as Callie was concerned. There was no way that Callie would break up a family, despite suspecting that he was also attracted to her – no way at all.

Chapter 4

Callie rubbed a spot on her forehead, just between her eyebrows where the pain seemed most concentrated, but it didn't help. Why had she drunk that free liqueur at the end of the meal? Never mix your drinks was her usual rule, but she'd broken it. All because Kate was flirting with the waiter and he insisted on bringing over the apple brandy, made by his family somewhere in Italy to a recipe only known by his grandfather or something equally unlikely, and with a kick like a horse. How many had they had? Callie couldn't remember past the second, but she was sure that she must have had at least one more.

Liqueurs were always a mistake for her, she knew that. Kate said she had no staying power when it came to alcohol, that she was a complete wuss, and Callie had to accept that her friend was almost certainly right. Callie was the one, throughout their friendship, who had always been the first to call a halt to a drinking session, usually by being sick. She also knew that because she didn't drink often, she would never get past that, but hey, she might be rubbish at drinking, but at least her liver was probably in good shape, even if it didn't feel that way at the moment.

There was a brief rap at the door and Linda, the practice manager, popped her head into the room. In her fifties, Linda treated the doctors in her practice like they were children and, God and Linda both knew, they certainly behaved worse than her children sometimes.

"Dear Lord, you look like death," she said encouragingly. "I hope you enjoyed yourself last night because you are certainly paying for it now."

"To be honest, I don't really remember."

Linda clucked disapprovingly.

"Well, that was a waste of good alcohol, then, wasn't it? I'll get you a coffee, a chocolate biscuit and a couple of paracetamol. Hopefully one of them will revive you."

Callie hoped so too, but she wasn't entirely convinced. She looked at her appointment list with trepidation, but they all seemed pretty benign, or at least, there were none of her usual heart-sink patients. She popped a mint in her mouth, straightened the forms on her desk which had somehow got out of alignment and pressed the buzzer for the first one, praying it would be something simple.

* * *

It wasn't until after her second cup of coffee that Callie began to feel better, and was less sharp with her poor patients who had done nothing to deserve her criticism or her possibly justified – but perhaps a little too blunt – judgements on their lifestyles. There was at least one poor man who had left her surgery convinced that if he didn't change his ways he'd be dead within a few months. Callie just hoped that the news inspired him to give up the ten pints and Indian takeaway every night and didn't cause him such despair that it drove him to even worse excess. And yes, she had to admit, she felt a complete hypocrite telling him to cut down on his drinking while knowing that she was having a go at him because she had had too much alcohol the night before.

Once the last patient had gone, Callie leant back with a sigh. At least she had finished early enough to take a brief break for lunch before visits. Then she remembered, horror of horrors, this afternoon was baby clinic. She had better get her act together before that, or all those screaming babies would completely finish her off. She washed her coffee mug in the sink, filled it with cold water and took a long draught. Maybe getting rehydrated wouldn't solve every problem, but at least it was making a start on one of them.

* * *

The District General Hospital had a mortuary set slightly apart from the main hospital buildings. The chapel of rest was marked clearly, but the mortuary entrance was to one side, plain and unmarked so that the general public would remain unaware of its purpose. No hospital wants to be too closely associated with death. Death is always seen as a failure in hospitals, an admission that doctors are not infallible.

Callie had to steel herself to push open the door and walk down the windowless corridor to the lift at the end. It was almost a year since she had been attacked in the subterranean mortuary and her dear friend and mentor Dr Ian Dunbar, the pathologist, had been killed. Although she had been back many times since, she would never feel as relaxed about visiting the mortuary as she had been before his death. A strangely quiet and peaceful place before, it was now filled with too many violent memories.

A locum pathologist, or rather a series of locum pathologists, had been working in the mortuary while the hospital tried to recruit a permanent consultant. Callie sorely missed Ian with his gentle, good-humoured ways and endless patience, happy to take the time to explain the meaning of his findings to doctors, nurses, relatives or policemen, in a way that they would understand. She still felt a small pang of sadness that he wouldn't be sitting at the desk, sipping Earl Grey tea and jabbing at the computer with two fingers, not least because the locum who was currently taking his place was so irritating.

Lucy Cavendish was a thin, colourless woman with a pointy face and a permanent look of discontent, probably because she felt her current position was beneath her. She had been forced to take locum posts after failing to find a permanent position where she had trained, and there was enough concern about her working practices at Hastings General to mean she was unlikely to be offered one here.

Callie walked down the corridor, checking the stockrooms and post-mortem room as she went by; they all seemed empty. When she got to the main office, she knocked on the door and poked her head inside the room. It too was deserted, and incredibly neat. Gone was the friendly disarray that Ian had worked in: the porcelain tea set, the biscuit barrel, the photos tacked to the board – some family, some gruesome examples of autopsies he had done – and the piles and piles of paper that were testament to his distrust of, and inability to use, the computer. Now, that computer seemed to be the only feature of the office; apart from a few textbooks on the shelf and a filing cabinet, there was nothing other than a desk and chair in the room, and certainly nothing of a personal nature.

Callie went back out into the corridor.

"Hello?" she called, hoping that someone was there and would hear her.

"Hey, Doc, how's it going?"

Callie turned to see Jim, the pathology technician, a skinny, wrinkled man, old before his time because of his addiction to cigarettes, who had more tattoos than teeth. Despite his unprepossessing appearance Callie liked him, and not just because he was a good source of information and gossip.

"Hello, Jim. All fine. How's it going here?" They both looked at the closed office door.

"Is Lucy around?"

"Dr Cavendish has gone to the medical meeting at the post grad centre. Can I help?" Jim had come out of the laundry room and was holding several clean sheets and stretcher linens for the patient trolleys.

"I just wanted to know when I was likely to get the report on the sudden death at the residential home," Callie asked, although they both knew she was really asking if Giles Townsend had been autopsied.

"I'm not sure if the report's finished yet." Jim gave her a look that told Callie that he knew the report wasn't finished, in fact it probably wasn't even started yet, and yes, he was aware that this delay was not really acceptable. Jim was experienced enough to know that reports needed to be done whilst the autopsy was still fresh in the pathologist's memory, even though Lucy Cavendish would have talked into a dictaphone whilst doing the procedure and would have most of the information she needed there. But if she didn't write the report until several days later, it would be hard to go back and check on something. "We've got a couple of outstanding cases from the hospital," he said, offering what was, at best, a very lame excuse.

"That's okay," Callie answered, although it wasn't; but it was hardly Jim's fault.

"And she did the autopsy on the auto-asphyxiation this morning," he added, which pleased Callie as she now didn't have to bring the subject up herself.

"Was everything as expected?"

"Absolutely." He nodded happily. "Textbook case of auto-erotic asphyxiation."

"And the kit's been sent to forensics?"

Jim looked embarrassed again.

"Dr Cavendish hasn't signed it off yet."

"Why ever not? Is she running tests of her own on it?"

"Not that I know of." Jim sighed. "She's so behind with the paperwork she hasn't even got everything together for the Hayes case and the inquest is next week."

Callie wasn't impressed.

"How can she be that far behind?"

Jim shrugged.

"I don't think she can be arsed to do it. It'll come back and bite her one day though. You mark my words."

Jim went off to do some work and Callie was left thinking that she hoped Lucy Cavendish did get caught out one day, just so long as it wasn't on one of her cases. Maybe she should speak to Mike Parton. Perhaps he would be able to get the evidence on Giles Townsend sent off faster.

* * *

Once she was back at her home, Callie would have liked nothing more than to pour herself a glass of ice-cold Pinot Grigio, but the thought of her morning hangover changed her mind and she made herself a mug of lemon and ginger tea instead. She took her tea and looked out of her living room windows at the view of Hastings Old Town below her.

It only took a few minutes for the view, and the tea, to work their magic and make her feel more relaxed and content. Studiously ignoring the flashing of her answer phone, she took her mug over to the sofa and switched on the television.

She had missed the six o'clock news and the local news had just started.

"Good evening." The programme anchor, a man in his thirties, smiled before putting on his serious face. "Tonight, an unexpected turn in the case of the Crown Prosecution Service Chief, Doreen Ponting, found over the drink-drive limit behind the wheel of her car last week."

A picture of a Honda Civic flashed up on the screen, parked in a wooded area with the driver's door open. There was a woman in the seat. The details of her face and body were heavily pixilated, but not heavily enough that you couldn't see that she was pretty much naked. The picture then cut to footage of Ms Ponting leaving the police station after she had been charged. She looked dreadful, as if, like Callie that morning, she had the hangover from hell.

"Vanessa Cardham is in Hastings," the anchor said, giving his audience the benefit of his best serious-but-interested look.

The camera cut to a young woman clutching a microphone and standing outside a good-sized family house.

"I'm standing outside the home of Doreen Ponting, the chief executive of East Sussex Crown Prosecution Service, who earlier made a statement regarding the charge made against her of drink driving."

The report cut to a pre-recorded segment.

Doreen Ponting was dressed in the formal and severe black suit that she always wore for work and she looked haggard, although not as haggard as she had looked when filmed leaving the police station. Callie thought she would have done better to soften her look a bit, even if just with a scarf or some jewellery. It might have got her more sympathy than the hard-nosed career-woman look. Callie was interested to see a middle-aged man standing behind her, immaculately dressed in a grey suit and blue tie, hands behind his back and staring resolutely at his feet. Mr Ponting, Callie decided, and if the situation was embarrassing for his wife, how hard must it be for him?

Doreen Ponting cleared her throat and rattled the paper she was holding.

"I am here today to tell you that I absolutely deny the charges against me and that I will strenuously fight them. I have been framed by someone for reasons as yet unknown, but I wish to make it clear that I have never driven whilst under the influence of drink or drugs, that I do not frequent places such as the one where I was found and that I am not in the habit of—" Her voice broke slightly, and her husband looked up briefly before returning to the examination of his shoes.

"I am not in the habit of sitting unclothed in my car. I believe the fact that the press were called before the police and that photographs were taken before the arrival of either support my belief that this was a carefully staged scene for the purpose of undermining my reputation, and I intend to find out who is responsible. Thank you." She turned and took her husband's hand, giving him a small, anxious smile.

There was a sudden outburst as journalists fired questions at her.

"Is your husband standing by you, Ms Ponting?"

"Who would want to set you up like this?"

"What does Mr Ponting think about dogging?"

Doreen Ponting turned back to the camera. Callie held her breath. She hoped the poor woman wasn't going to answer that final question.

"I have put a lot of bad people away in my time," she answered, and Callie heaved a sigh of relief. "I think it is highly likely that one of them is trying to humiliate me as an act of revenge or to prevent me from continuing to prosecute them. I want to be absolutely clear to that person that I will find them and that I won't be intimidated." Once again Doreen Ponting turned away from the camera and walked firmly up her front steps, back ramrod straight, husband in tow, and closed the door against the rush of further questions being hurled after her.

A good performance, but was it good enough and was it the truth? Callie had no doubt that there were indeed many people who would like to get their own back on the prosecutor, but to set this up they would have had to get her drunk and drive her to the dogging site in her own car and then undress her. That seemed an awfully difficult set of actions to complete without her knowing it was happening and without anyone witnessing it. Surely it was more likely that she had gone there under her own steam and met up with someone who perhaps had given her some more alcohol or drugs? Callie wasn't convinced Ms Ponting was completely innocent and what was more, in that brief moment when her husband looked up, Callie was pretty sure he didn't think so either.

Chapter 5

Morning surgery had been something of a nightmare and Callie was cross and running late as she hurried into the office and collided with Richard, the latest new registrar to do his GP training with them. As they both stooped to pick up the files and reports that had fallen everywhere as a result of the collision, Richard apologised profusely. Several times.

"I'm s-s-so sorry, Dr Hughes," he stuttered, blushing dreadfully. "It was all my fault."

"Please call me Callie, Richard, and I think you'll find it was my fault for rushing through the door without looking. You just happened to be standing there."

Callie's admission of guilt didn't stop him from apologising.

"Sorry Dr Hu... Callie," he said quickly, as if he wasn't at ease using her first name. "I wondered if I could have a word, but obviously you won't have time now. I quite understand."

Having answered his own request, he turned to go and Callie had to call him back.

"Richard! Of course I have time." She lied. "What was it you wanted to talk to me about?"

"A patient," he replied tentatively.

"Yes?" She had to bite her lip to stop herself from asking him to narrow it down a bit. She had more than two thousand patients on her list so she could hardly be expected to guess which one it was. She honestly wondered if Richard would ever make it as a GP.

"A, um… Mr Herring," he finally managed to say and fished around in the bag he was carrying, pulling out a very thick wad of paper that was, she saw to her dismay, a printout of Mr Herring's notes. She glanced at her watch. She really didn't have time to discuss Mr Herring's long and convoluted interactions with herself and pretty much every other doctor in the practice and a fair number at the hospital as well. It had to be said that Mr Herring was well known to health service providers across Hastings and beyond.

"I was trying to make sense of all these notes. He seems to have had an awful lot of tests for, well, many different diseases but there don't seem to be many actual diagnoses in his past history."

"No, well, that's because we've never actually found anything wrong with Mr Herring other than acute hypochondria."

"Oh." Richard looked disappointed and went back to the sheaf of papers in his hand. "But–"

"Richard, you were right, I really don't have time for this. Mr Herring is the bane of all our lives. He Googles symptoms that he thinks he has and comes in with printouts of diseases he wants to be tested for. He is single-handedly costing the NHS hundreds of thousands of pounds a year, and no one has ever found anything wrong with him."

Richard looked crestfallen and that, in turn, made Callie feel guilty.

"Look," she continued, hoping to cheer him up a bit. "He's a great patient to discuss with your clinical supervisor, might even make a good case study."

Richard visibly brightened and Callie hurried away to grab a coffee and make a start on her paperwork before he could manage to get out so much as a thank you.

* * *

Armed with a list of visits and a tuna salad sandwich, Callie went into her consulting room to make a quick phone call before leaving the surgery. Much as her colleagues understood her desire to run her two jobs in parallel, Callie was not unaware that her police work often meant she had to leave them, and her patients, in the lurch. There had been many occasions when visits did not get done or surgeries had to be covered by others. She tried, as much as possible, to keep her police work out of their sight as she found it the best way to avoid eye-rolls from the other GPs and lectures from Dr Grantham, the senior partner, about it being time to confine herself to just one career and do it well rather than flitting about and letting people down all the time.

That was why she was sitting in her consulting room where she could unobtrusively make a call to Mike Parton, knowing that lunchtimes were often a good time to catch him in his office.

"Hello, Mike? It's Callie here. I just wondered if you knew whether or not the paraphernalia from the Townsend case had been sent off?"

There was a slight pause before Mike answered.

"I was about to say I assume so, but—"

"Lucy Cavendish isn't known for her efficiency." Callie finished for him.

"Quite. Can I ask, do you know something about this?"

"I did hear from a pretty reliable source" — Callie knew that Parton would guess exactly who that source was — "that she might not have signed the release forms for them to go to forensics yet."

They both knew that with the backlog of work that had built up since the forensic department had been put out to tender – a tender which had been won by a quote that was naïve at best – meant that it was hard enough to get the evidence together in time for inquests and trials without the pathologist adding in extra delays.

"Thank you, Dr Hughes. I'll get onto it right away," Parton said as he quickly hung up, clearly keen to do just as he said.

* * *

Callie was jumpy throughout evening surgery, half-expecting to get a tirade of abuse from Lucy Cavendish for interfering in one of her cases, but there were no calls. Either the pathologist didn't care, or she was just biding her time to have a proper go at Callie somewhere public, like the inquest.

Mike Parton had called earlier to tell Callie that he had dropped off the gear at the police forensic laboratory and requested the tests on behalf of the coroner's office. He confided in Callie that not only was she slow, but that he didn't think the locum pathologist was particularly thorough.

"If it wasn't for me and Mr Rickard checking that everything that should be done has been, I sometimes think we would get to the inquests without any idea as to how people died, and still be just as much in the dark afterwards."

Callie knew that Mr Rickard, a pedantic and very thorough solicitor who was now the local coroner, must hate being presented with incomplete or slapdash evidence. No wonder Parton was looking a bit strained these days. It was bad enough having to make sure his own work was in perfect order without having to double check the pathologist's work as well.

Having completed her paperwork, Callie finally left the surgery and stopped off at the supermarket to buy some chicken breasts, mushrooms and fresh pasta, along with the makings of a salad, some milk and fresh bread. She was just debating with herself the best way to cook the chicken when she parked at the end of the lane where she lived. Her home was the top flat, or penthouse apartment as the estate agent had insisted on calling it, created when a large Edwardian house was divided into six separate flats in the nineties. She was lucky that conversions then were much more sympathetic to the architectural style and retained many of the original features, unlike earlier examples she had seen. In the sixties and seventies developers had been far too quick to rip out fireplaces and stick up stud walls straight through elaborate cornices and ceiling roses.

The house was situated at the end of a narrow lane that led to nowhere except the cliff-top park, and it had magnificent views over Hastings Old Town and to the sea beyond. It was the views from her large living room windows that had sold the flat to Callie several years earlier when she had come to live and work in the town. Some people might have considered the house's position a little isolated, but Callie liked the feeling of peace and separation from the town whilst knowing that it was still within easy walking distance. It was coming home again, up the steep steps and twittens, the walkways and lanes that turn Hastings into a maze, that was a chore, although at least during the day she had the East Cliff lift and could then walk through the country park to her home. The lift stopped at six o'clock, but Callie wouldn't want to walk across the cliffs on her own at night, anyway. There were sometimes flashers in the copses, and it would be downright embarrassing if she recognised one as a patient.

The phone was ringing as she entered the flat and, even as she picked it up, Callie knew it was a mistake. She'd ignored several messages from her mother, knowing that if it was anything important her father would have contacted her, and suspecting that her mother was trying to set her up with yet another blind date.

"Hi Ma, how are you?" she said, trying for a level of brightness she wasn't feeling.

"We're both fine, thank you, although how we'd let you know if we weren't, I don't know. You should return my calls occasionally." Her mother was frustrated more than angry, and she had every right to be, Callie knew.

"Sorry, I've just been so busy..."

"You are always busy. And yes, I do know that you have a responsible job, two responsible jobs, but you need to find time for your family."

"Sorry, Ma. I know." Callie was suitably penitent. "What can I do for you?"

There was an ominous pause, and Callie knew she wasn't going to like what her mother had to say.

"You remember Rita and George's son?"

"Rita and George?" Callie didn't even remember them, let alone their son, and she definitely didn't like the way this conversation was going.

"You know, they own the oast house in the village down the road. Edward went to Harrow and then up to Cambridge to read maths. You must remember him."

Callie certainly did. Teddy at sixteen had been pretty unprepossessing – pale, spotty and underweight. He had sported a permanent scowl. Not that Callie had necessarily been drawn to the sporty or buff boys who thought so much of themselves, but she had her standards as a teenager, and Teddy was well below the line. He also had no idea how to talk to girls, or boys for that matter. He could really only talk maths.

"Anyway, whether or not you remember him, he's back staying with his parents at the moment and I've invited them over for dinner tomorrow night and I'll need you there to even the numbers up."

Her mother's age-old excuse when she was setting her daughter up with yet another supposedly eligible bachelor was that she needed Callie to come so that there would be an even number of men and women at the table. Quite why that was so important, Callie had never really understood.

"But—"

"Rita was saying that it's really quite trying having your child boomerang back to live with you at this stage of your life, so we are doing them a big favour just getting him out of the house for an evening."

"Yes but his parents are coming too, so it's not like you're giving them a break."

"Well, of course they don't need a break from him, darling, he's their son, but they are worried that he doesn't get out enough."

"So, why does that need me to be there?" Callie knew that the whole point of the dinner party was for her to meet Edward, but she wasn't going to roll over that easily.

"Well, he won't want to come to dinner with a bunch of old fogeys, will he?"

Actually, from what Callie remembered of Teddy, he probably wouldn't notice.

"You are there to add a bit of glamour, darling."

Callie desperately tried to think of an excuse not to go.

"Please, darling, Rita really is at her wits end and I promised. You wouldn't want me to break that promise, would you?"

With a sigh, Callie accepted the invitation.

Chapter 6

He leaned back in the hot water that was bubbling around him, took another sip of his whisky and looked up at the stars, or the few stars that were visible. Even on a cool night he loved sitting naked in a hot tub and looking at the stars, but the light pollution and clouds in Kent meant that there were not very many to be seen. He remembered a similar night in the Cayman Islands. He had been able to see hundreds, thousands, or maybe even hundreds of thousands then. Perhaps he should take it as a sign that it was time to cut his losses here and go? Go to the Caymans where he had a fair-sized fortune stashed under another name. He could even change his identity there, and hide from his money-grabbing bitch of a wife. Stupid cow, threatening to divorce him and take him for every penny. Did she think he wasn't prepared for her trying to do exactly that?

He sipped his whisky and idly scratched his balls. He should stay and fight the allegations against him, which he could do successfully, he knew, in time. The problem was that the chief exec was itching to get rid of him anyway, so he wouldn't be given time, any more than he would be given access to the system, so that he could prove it wasn't him who had sent those emails. Unless – he thought for a moment – that Friday night when the emails had been sent, was when he was on the train home, drunk as a skunk as befitted the end of the working week. Could he have sent them? A massive act of self-destruction? He didn't think so. Particularly not the one about screwing the CEO's wife. I mean, she must be at least forty. Well-preserved, but older than anyone he had ever shagged. So, he wouldn't have sent that one, would he? Even if he had sent the ones about illegal dealing. Which he didn't, obviously.

Someone else must have set him up. No shortage of candidates there. Could someone have lifted his phone and sent them while he was out of it on the train? They would have needed his thumbprint to open the phone – surely, he would have woken up if they did that? He thought for a moment and took another sip from his drink. God, it didn't taste as good as he expected it to. It was supposed to be one of the best single malts money could buy. Maybe the bitch had tipped it out and put some cheap shit in there as a *fuck you* gesture. He wouldn't put it past her. He wouldn't put anything past her now. She had been furious when he was sacked for gross misconduct. Furious that she hadn't been able to start divorce proceedings before the humiliation, not to mention before his income took such a turn for the worse.

He was beginning to feel a bit fuzzy headed. Perhaps he'd had too much to drink? Well, why not? After all, he didn't have to go to work in the morning, did he?

He snorted with laughter and took another defiant gulp of the foul-tasting whisky and drained the glass, shouting, "Up yours, you, stupid cunt!" He'd have to make plans tomorrow. Plans to cut loose. Forget the bloody job and the bastards that worked there, especially the cunt who had sent those sodding emails in his name, and forget his stupid cow of a wife who had no loyalty to him, let alone love for him. No loyalty at all.

Christ, he felt tired, perhaps he should go to bed. He closed his eyes momentarily and slid down in the water, floating on the bubbles. So tired, so sleepy, he didn't feel the hand stroking his forehead and pushing his head gently under the water.

Chapter 7

Callie was deeply asleep when the phone next to her bed rang, and it took several rings before she realised that the sound was real, not part of her dream. She reached out, groggily, and pulled the receiver under the covers without even opening her eyes. After years of disturbed nights, some doctors had perfected the art of becoming immediately fully awake and alert, but not Callie. She was never going to get used to being woken in the middle of the night.

"Yes?" was all she managed to say, and even that was muffled by the bedclothes.

"Dr Hughes?"

"Yes?" Callie sighed, and struggled to sit up. This wasn't a wrong number or drunken friend she could cut off. This was work, so she could give up any idea of going back to sleep.

"There's been a sudden death out at Cazeley Village. A drowning at a house called Compton's Cazeley in Barn Lane."

"Drowning?"

"In the swimming pool."

"Oh." That was unusual in itself; Hastings was not the sort of area where swimming pools were commonplace. "Have you called the coroner's officer?"

"Yes, he's already on his way but he asked me to wait until a civilised hour before giving you a call, let you get a bit more sleep."

Callie managed to get the receiver back in the cradle, checked the clock, and lay there for a moment or two, muttering and collecting her thoughts. It was a Saturday morning, for goodness sake. How could they call six o'clock a civilised hour, even if she could see from the dawn light creeping through the chink in the curtains that the sun was pretty much up, and she could hear the infuriatingly cheerful singing of the birds? Or rather, the awful squawking of the seagulls. At least she didn't have a morning surgery booked. If cancelling a clinic during the week made her unpopular, then missing a Saturday one caused serious upset. Even a home-made cake, always supposing she knew how to make one, wouldn't be enough to placate her colleagues. With a groan, she threw the duvet back and crawled out of bed.

* * *

Compton's Cazeley turned out to be an impressive detached nineteen-thirties house, in a quiet spot outside the picturesque village of Cazeley. There were several cars parked in the ample driveway as Callie drove in: a small black and silver, almost feminine 4x4, a 'look-at-me-I'm-richer-than-you' silver Bentley, waxed and buffed to shiny perfection, and an even less discreet marked police car. There was also an ambulance, with its rear doors open, but no one inside. Mike Parton's car was furthest from the house and Callie parked next to him. She checked her face in the mirror before getting out, just to be sure that every hair was in the right place despite the early hour and the rush. There was nothing she hated more than to look in any way dishevelled in public. Callie wasn't sure whether or not to go to the front door, but saw Mike Parton waiting for her by an open gate to the back garden and followed him through it.

There were a cluster of people around the swimming pool as Callie walked round the side of the house with Parton. A constable was standing next to a man in his early sixties, Callie guessed, who either had a problem with his blood pressure or was extremely angry. Or both. The two ambulance men stood a little apart, probably waiting for someone to tell them they could go, because it was clear that they were no longer needed. A second constable, a very capable-looking young woman, was standing next to the body of a man lying face up next to the pool.

The day was already warm for the time of year, the sun was quickly evaporating any water around the corpse, and the tiles were only faintly darker underneath him. Callie began her examination as she walked towards the body. She could see that he was a small man, verging on the under-weight and completely naked, the area usually covered by swimming trunks pale in comparison to his well-tanned torso. She continued her visual check as she crouched down beside the man. Parton and the female constable moved a few steps away, to give her space and so that the coroner's officer could be briefed on what had already been established. The constable had taken out her notebook in case she needed to refer to it as she made her report.

"The victim is a Mr Adrian Cole, aged forty-four according to the house owner Mr Wendlesham." The constable nodded towards the choleric man.

"Sir," he said sharply. "I'm Sir Geoffrey Wendlesham, not Mr."

"Sir Geoffrey Wendlesham." The constable corrected herself in a long-suffering voice.

"And he was staying here?" Parton asked.

"No! He bloody well wasn't staying here," Sir Geoffrey interjected, unable to keep quiet any longer. "He's just done this to embarrass me, as if he hadn't already done that."

Parton raised an eyebrow and Callie went back to the body and, like the ambulance personnel, listened intently to the conversation. This was obviously a more interesting start to the day than they had been expecting.

"I sacked him last week for gross misconduct. Had to come back from Antigua to do it. Good job my wife stayed over there, wouldn't want her to see this." Wendlesham paused for a moment to look at the body in disgust. "He knew he'd never work again, at least not in the financial sector, not after what he did. So, it is entirely understandable that he chose to commit suicide, but he didn't have to bloody well do it in my swimming pool!"

"Right, Sir Geoffrey, if you could go inside with the constable?" Parton nodded at the policeman standing next to him. "I'll be with you in a moment to take a statement."

Surprisingly, Wendlesham went with the constable with only a slight harrumph to signify his disgust at the situation he had woken to find himself in.

"If you could continue your report, please." Parton said to the remaining constable once the house owner was out of earshot.

"Mr, Sir, Wendlesham." Sir Geoffrey's correction seemed to have flustered the poor woman. "He came out onto the terrace at oh five hundred hours and spotted something floating in the pool. When he got a bit closer, he could see it was a body and he used a pole to steer the body to the side and pull it out of the pool. Once he realised the man was dead he called us and the ambulance. That was at five fifteen."

Callie had finished her visual check and was pulling on some gloves.

"Why did you call out the doc?" Parton asked the constable. "The ambulance crew could have pronounced death."

"Yes, but when there's going to be an inquest, I just thought it would be best to be sure there wasn't anything untoward." She explained and Parton nodded approvingly, even though it was more likely her concern about Sir Geoffrey that was the cause of her caution.

"Okay. That's good. You can never be too careful."

"Can you give me a hand please?" Callie asked and they both turned to look at her. She had pulled the body towards her, so that she could check the back. Parton came over and held the body steady so that Callie could get a closer look at something she had seen.

"I think we need to get a team out here," she told him, pointing to visible cuts and scratches on the shoulders and back of the legs.

Parton hesitated.

"Couldn't that have happened when he was pulled out of the pool?"

"It's possible, but there's some dirt in the deeper cuts, and he's had some facial trauma too. It looks as though it all occurred post-mortem but you how it is, Mike," she said as she pulled off her gloves. "Just in case he didn't go voluntarily into the pool, or there was some kind of fight. This could end up getting messy with blame being hurled in all directions. We're going to need a full forensic work-up for the inquest, no matter what."

Parton sighed and nodded his agreement to the PC who walked towards the front of the house, reaching for her radio as she walked.

"I'll ring the mortuary, give them the heads-up and make sure they do a full tox screen as well, if you want to let Sir Geoffrey know what's going on," Callie continued.

Parton nodded again and reluctantly went over to the house to break the news that there would soon be a full team of crime scene examiners and several more policemen stomping all over the garden and, quite possibly, the house as well.

* * *

Sir Geoffrey had clearly not taken the news well, Callie could hear his raised voice from the front of the house as she leant against her car and waited for the crime scene team and CID to arrive.

"What do you mean we can't refuse permission?" rang out from the open windows.

She couldn't make out Parton's quieter, more measured response, but the 'That's bloody ridiculous, I'm getting onto my solicitor. And the Chief Constable. He's a personal friend, you know,' he got in response was loud and clear, and she heard the door bang as they presumably went further inside the house. The two ambulance men pulled a face at her and closed the rear doors of their vehicle, happy that there was nothing for them to do and they could go back to the ambulance station and clock off their shift only a little later than they should have done, with a great story to tell their colleagues. There was no doubt – if Mr Cole had committed suicide in his boss's pool to wind him up, he had succeeded.

As she watched the ambulance pull out of the driveway, and the white forensics van pull in, Callie wondered who would come from CID. Realistically, she knew that it was unlikely to be anyone senior; this was probably a very minor case, with the likelihood that any damage to the body that occurred post-mortem would warrant no further action. But, if all was quiet, or Sir Geoffrey rattled enough cages, they might get someone senior, someone like Detective Inspector Steve Miller. She wasn't sure if she wanted it to be Steve Miller or not after the embarrassment of seeing him, and Jeffries, at the auto-asphyxiation.

She heard the sound of a car approaching and turned to see Miller's silver Avensis turn into the drive. As soon as it had stopped, the passenger door opened and Jeffries got out.

"Watcha got for us then, Doc?"

Callie sighed. One thing was certain, she might miss Miller if she never saw him again, but she wouldn't miss Bob Jeffries.

"Male Caucasian. Probable death by drowning, maybe suicide but there are some complicating factors," she said as she approached the car.

"Like what?" Miller asked as he too got out of the car and joined them. Callie turned and led them towards the swimming pool, where the female constable was setting up a perimeter using crime scene tape to prevent anyone else from approaching the body until the crime scene investigators had finished work on the site. There were flashes behind her as photographs were taken of the body in situ.

"Signs that the body has been manhandled. It looks as though it happened after death, and the injuries may even have occurred when the body was hauled out of the pool, but I can't rule out the possibility of them having happened around the time of death."

They had reached the edge of the taped-off area and Colin Brewer, the crime scene manager dressed in his full forensic outfit, came over to them, possibly to speak to Miller but Callie suspected it was more to make sure they didn't come any closer without suiting up. Mike Parton joined them, having left Sir Geoffrey to make another call of complaint.

"If you could just let us finish, sir, then you can get a closer look at the body."

Miller nodded and turned to Callie.

"Is there a note, do you know?"

She shrugged and looked at Colin and Mike.

"There isn't one here, but he may have left one at his home." Colin added.

"This isn't where he lived then?" Miller asked, surprised.

"Er, no. And thereby hangs another complication," Callie told him. "This is the home of his CEO, or ex-CEO who sacked our victim a few days ago."

"Explains a lot," Jeffries said.

"He could have left a note on his laptop, or phone," Callie said. "Or an email maybe, as it was some outrageous emails, according to Sir Geoffrey, that got him sacked."

"No note, no phone and no clothes with his body," Colin said.

Callie kicked herself; she hadn't thought of that.

"In his car?" she suggested.

"And no car that we've found yet. Course it could be out there, parked in the lanes somewhere, with his clothes as you suggest, Dr Hughes." He indicated the surrounding countryside.

"And he walked here in the buff?" Jeffries queried.

"Or someone dropped him here and left," Miller added as he looked round. "Either way, we'll need to search the area. Colin, do you have any idea how he got into the grounds?"

Colin pointed to a hedge where some white suited crime scene examiners were working.

"It's possible he came through there, some of the branches have been broken as if someone has forced their way through."

At that moment, they heard another car arriving and turned around. To Callie's dismay she recognised a local reporter getting out of the battered car. Sir Geoffrey was definitely not going to like that. Miller sent the constable to make sure the journalist didn't get anywhere near the scene.

"How on earth did he get here so fast?" Callie asked.

"Tipped off by one of the neighbours, I wouldn't wonder," Colin said, but Callie couldn't see any neighbours who would be close enough to know anything was going on. She turned back just as the crime scene tech who had been taking photographs of Cole's body stepped away, giving Miller and Jeffries a clear view of the dead man for the first time.

"Blimey, he didn't have much to write home about, did he?" Jeffries was clearly looking at the genital area. "No wonder he topped himself."

Chapter 8

The Old Vicarage, Callie's childhood home, was a beautiful house – symmetrical and graceful. Now that it was spring, its dove grey stucco was festooned with pale, lilac-blue Wisteria blossoms. These Callie loved even more than the twisted, woody stems that clung to the walls around the front door and ground floor windows, covered with lime green leaf sprays and silver, velvety seed pods all summer. There were two cars parked outside; her father's aging Volvo, and her mother's small hatchback, a car she religiously changed for a new one, the same model and even, usually, the same colour, every other year. Callie stopped her sporty little Audi TT next to it and paused for a moment before getting out. Callie had always loved this house, it held so many memories of growing up.

With a sigh, she got out of the car and headed for the front door. Dinner with her parents, and even worse, being set up as an almost blind date with a neighbour's son, was not how Callie wanted to spend her Saturday evening, but she knew she had to put a brave face on it for her mother's sake.

She had come armed with a bunch of freesias, her mother's favourite flowers, and a box of chocolates. She had also made sure she was a little early so that she could offer to help. Not that her mother would need it: Diana Hughes always had absolutely everything under perfect control. Callie wondered if she would ever be the same, or at least be able to have a dinner party and not manage to forget a vital ingredient or burn the main course.

"Darling, how lovely, my favourite." Diana air-kissed Callie on each cheek, so that she could avoid smudging her make-up. "Can you put them in a vase for me? Charles, get the poor girl a drink."

Diana hurried back into the kitchen to stir something and Callie smiled at her father. He was looking better than he had in years. Perhaps he was finally over the shock of no longer being a consultant orthopaedic surgeon and settling into his well-earned retirement.

"How are you, Dad?" she asked. "You're looking well."

"Oh, I'm full of beans, thanks. How about you? Here, let me take those." He took the chocolates and followed her into the utility room, where she grabbed a vase, added water and put the flowers into it.

"Fine, thanks."

Once Callie had found a place for the flowers in the living room and made her obligatory offer to help in the kitchen, which was refused, she settled in the immaculate living room with her father and a glass of perfectly chilled white wine.

"How's work?" her father asked.

"Much the same as ever; two cases for the coroner, an accidental and a suicide." She felt strangely reluctant to go into the details of Giles Townsend's little 'accident' with her father. Masturbation was hardly a suitable dinner party topic.

"Ah, yes. There's been quite a bit in the papers about those. Were you involved with the case of the crown prosecution lady, the one who was found over the limit?"

"No, she was picked up closer to Eastbourne, so they took her there."

"That's a strange case, isn't it?"

"Very, I just can't understand why people take risks like that."

The doorbell rang and they both headed into the spacious hall to greet the new arrivals as Diana opened the door to them.

"Rita! George! Come in, come in. How lovely to see you, and this must be Teddy. Gosh, it's been years since we last saw you, Teddy. You haven't changed a bit!"

Callie was surprised by how her mother could lie so fluently because Teddy had changed considerably since the last time she had seen him. He had filled out. A lot. In fact, he had filled out and overflowed, but under all the fat, the scowl was still the same. Callie had the feeling that Teddy wasn't there of his own volition. Like her, he'd rather have been almost anywhere else.

"He prefers to be called Edward these days." Rita corrected Diana.

"Of course, Edward, such a lovely name. You remember my daughter, Calliope?"

Callie cringed.

"Hello, actually–" A glare from Diana stopped Callie from adding that she preferred to be called Callie these days. She could tell from the twinkle in her father's eye that he knew exactly what she had been about to say.

* * *

After pre-dinner drinks in the living room, with Edward – or Teddy, as he would always be to Callie, regardless of his preferences – managing only monosyllabic responses to all his mother's efforts to draw him into conversation, they moved into the dining room. Callie was firmly placed between Teddy and Charles. She would happily have spent the entire meal talking to her father, but dinner party rules meant that she had to alternately converse with her father and Teddy. His terse replies in the living room had informed her that he now worked for British Telecom, and his mother had expanded on this to make out that he practically ran the company.

"Do you like working for British Telecom?" she asked him. A pretty boring start, but hopefully safe, Callie thought.

"Not really." Teddy didn't even look up from his plate of homemade chicken liver pate and red onion marmalade.

"Are you staying with your parents long?" She tried again.

"Don't know."

It was going to be a long dinner, Callie thought as she passed him the breadbasket, again.

With perseverance, Callie managed to discover that Teddy had been living with a girlfriend, but they had split up recently and she had kept the flat. That was why he had to move in with his parents. Apparently, he had initiated the split, but Callie was pretty sure he was lying, despite his mother chipping in that she had never thought his ex-girlfriend was good enough for him. She also found out, in snippets whilst they ate rack of lamb and later, pot au chocolat, that he didn't run BT, he was just head of a small bit of the IT department and he felt the job was beneath him.

The more general dinner party conversation drifted round to the sensational arrest of the head of the CPS and from there to the death of Giles Townsend, with Callie studiously avoiding saying anything that could be a breach of confidence.

"Never liked the man," George said, with a mouthful of roast potato. Callie was interested to know that he was acquainted with Giles Townsend. She had forgotten, if she ever knew, that George was a lawyer of some sort.

"Oh, really? Why's that?" Charles asked him.

"Always something a bit unpleasant about him. The way he treated the women who worked for him. When he was with a firm I knew in London, staff turnover was always way too high."

"You think he might have" – Callie searched for words that would convey her meaning without being too coarse for the dinner table – "over-stepped the mark with them?"

"Exactly. A bit hands on, if you know what I mean. Used to like the office girlies to deliver his briefs to his flat and would open the door with nothing on, that sort of thing."

With difficulty, Callie ignored his offensive reference to the administration clerks and legal secretaries as 'office girlies'.

"I'm amazed there weren't complaints."

"I think there were. At least one, I heard, but they managed to hush it up. Think they were glad when he decided to relocate to Hastings." George stuffed a large lump of lamb in his mouth. "Or was it after he moved down here that he got reported to the regulatory authority?" he asked himself, chewing thoughtfully.

Callie thought back to the day she had gone to Giles Townsend's flat to pronounce death. The person who had found his body had been a young woman who had been sent round from his practice so perhaps he was still doing the same thing. She suppressed a shudder of disgust. No person should ever have to put up with that sort of behaviour from his or her employer, or anyone else for that matter.

* * *

It was much to Callie's relief that Teddy insisted, soon after she had helped her mother serve coffee, that he had to go and finish some work. His parents said that they would stay and walk back when they were ready and Callie realised that Teddy had driven them there, despite only living a few hundred yards away. Rita and George didn't stay that much later, and Diana retired to bed with a headache once they had gone, leaving Callie and her father to tackle the clearing up, as they had always done after Diana's dinner parties.

"I don't think I need to ask what you think of Teddy, do I?" Charles asked as he handed her a dish to dry.

"No. I don't think you do." Callie answered with a smile. "I think even Ma realises that it's not going to be a match made in heaven, or anywhere else for that matter. I'm just hoping she'll give the whole husband search a rest for a while now."

"No guarantee of that, you know. It is your mother's mission in life, after all."

And she knew he was right.

* * *

On Sunday mornings, Callie's routine was to clean her flat and then go for brunch and a read of the Sunday papers at a café in the High Street, The Land of Green Ginger. Sometimes Kate joined her, particularly if either of them had had a date the night before, which neither had in this case, because Callie certainly wasn't counting Teddy as a date, but she knew Kate would want to hear all about the dinner party, so she wasn't surprised to see her friend waiting for her.

"How was the dinner party from hell?" was the first thing Kate asked.

"Just your average degree of awfulness."

"Teddy not a dream boat then?"

"That would be a definite no."

"Did he insist you all eat in silence to aid your digestion or bore you to death by holding forth on his pet subject? Come on, I want all the gory details. Your mother has the unerring ability to pick the world's most unsuitable men for you."

"He was just plain boring. Nothing interesting about him at all. Isn't that a terrible thing to say about anybody?"

"Gosh, yes. Not even really fit then?"

"No." Callie laughed. "No. I don't wish to be unkind, but he was" – she hesitated, searching for a description – "large."

"At least you always get a decent meal at your mother's."

"I am grateful for small mercies." Callie smiled. "And the conversation, other than with Teddy, was interesting."

"Oh, yes! I knew there'd be something. Tell me all." Kate perked up.

"You'll be able to answer this. If there was a complaint to the regulatory authority, or whatever it is called for solicitors…" She looked questioningly at Kate.

"Solicitors Regulation Authority, or SRA," Kate replied. "What sort of complaint?"

"Say, about someone sexually harassing his office staff… would there be a record of it? A record that I might be able to get hold of?"

"That would depend on whether it went anywhere," Kate admitted. "The great and the good in law are pretty experienced at covering things up when one of their own transgresses. Why?" Her eyes were twinkling; there was nothing Kate enjoyed more than a gossip about one of her colleagues. "And, more importantly, who are we talking about? Teddy? Your dinner party is beginning to sound more interesting."

"No, no, just something I heard about Giles Townsend."

"Oh, him. I wouldn't put anything past that toad. What's he supposed to have done to get reported?"

"Persuaded the young female staff to deliver his papers to his home and then opened the door in the buff, I think."

Kate pulled a face.

"God! Just thinking about it is enough to put you off your breakfast." Kate took a hefty bite of her toast, so it presumably hadn't really affected her appetite. "Men like that should be publicly shamed. They had the right idea in the middle ages, with stocks and pillories."

Callie wasn't overly keen on medieval punishments but tying a sexual predator like Giles Townsend to a pillory and pelting him with rotten tomatoes didn't sound like a bad idea.

"Well, if one of them complained and it was upheld," Kate continued, "there should be a record of the hearing and any punishment, but if the case was dropped before it actually got to a hearing, which I suspect was the case, it would be much harder to get hold of anything."

"Why do you think it was dropped?"

"Because we would probably all know about it if not. He might even have been struck off, or suspended for a while. Anyway, I'll have a trawl on the internet and see if I can find anything for you."

"Thank you. Don't go to too much trouble, it won't make any difference to the coroner's case, but it just gives me a more complete picture." Callie didn't look as if she really wanted a more complete picture.

"Not at all, I'm more than a little interested to know the answer, now that you've brought it up. And on a more serious note, if he did do it and the bigwigs of the SRA let him get away with it, not that I'm saying they did, I'd very much like to shake things up a bit. Make them worry."

"Wouldn't that be bad for your career?" Callie knew her friend sometimes acted recklessly in this way.

"Possibly, but sometimes us professional women need to give the establishment something to worry over, don't you think?"

Callie wasn't sure that she agreed.

"Now what else have you been up to?" Kate continued. "Any more salacious gossip?"

Callie told her about the probable suicide out at Compton's Cazeley.

"Wow! That's quite a way to get your own back."

"I know. Vindictive. The poor man will never be able to use his pool without feeling guilty about the colleague he drove to suicide."

"He probably deserves the guilt." Kate was always less forgiving than Callie. They both thought for a moment and sipped their drinks. Kate closed her eyes and soaked up the late morning sun streaming through the café windows. "Did they find his car?"

"Yes, it was parked in the entrance to a field a short distance away, keys in the ignition, but there were no clothes inside."

"He drove there buck naked?" Kate laughed. "Imagine if he'd been stopped by the police on the way."

"I know." Callie felt bad for smiling. After all, if he had been stopped by the police, he might still be alive.

Chapter 9

On Wednesday morning, Callie finally got to see the autopsy report on Giles Townsend, which came in the same postal delivery as Adrian Cole's. Clearly the pathologist was sending out her reports in batches. Perhaps Mike had given her a dressing-down, or better still, the coroner had. Despite having received both the reports in the morning, she wasn't able to look at them until lunchtime, and it was a late lunch, because morning surgery had overrun. It was a rare occasion when Callie was able to help out her colleagues by taking some of their patients; in fact it was more often the other way round, so she really couldn't complain when Hugh Grantham, the senior partner, rang in sick and his patients had to be divided between the remaining doctors.

"I hope he really is sick," Gauri Sinha muttered as she finally appeared in the office at the end of what had obviously been a fraught surgery. "I was only running slightly late until Richard interrupted because he was worried about a patient, and when I went in to see how I could help, it was that stupid Mr Herring. He spent so long complaining about the fact that it was five minutes past his appointment time when Richard called him through, that I never got the chance to sort out what was really wrong with him and I was still forty minutes late with the next patient."

"Oh dear."

"I told Richard not to worry me with patients like Mr Herring again." Gauri stomped off to the kitchen to make herself some coffee.

Callie gave Linda, the practice manager, a guilty look, because when she had checked the list of her extras she had spotted Mr Herring's name and agreed to take more than her fair share of the others provided she didn't get him. It seemed that it had been a good call.

"Poor Richard."

"I'd better take him down some coffee and try and rebuild his fragile ego," Linda said with a sigh.

Callie picked up the autopsy reports to take down to her consulting room, on the grounds that she was less likely to be disturbed there, but she was stopped by Linda before she had even left the office.

"Don't forget that Hugh's visits have to be covered as well," she said as she handed Callie a list of names and addresses.

"Right." Callie took the list and looked at it with dismay.

"I know it's one of your half days, but the others have to get back for evening surgery, so count this as one of the days you pay back all the times you have been called out by the police and they have had to do your visits for you."

Callie really couldn't argue about it. It was true that Gauri Sinha in particular had done an awful lot of visits for her, so she took the list without further complaint and went down to her room with it as well as both post-mortem reports. She wouldn't have too much time to look at them if she was going to manage to do all the visits before midnight. For once, Callie was pleased that the reports were perfunctory and there was nothing unexpected in either of them.

Giles Townsend had died of asphyxiation as a result of having been hung by the neck. He had small amounts of cocaine, sildenafil and amyl nitrite in his system along with quite a lot of alcohol. What a mix, Callie thought. Poppers, coke and Viagra. He had slight atherosclerosis and left ventricular hypertrophy suggesting that his blood pressure needed better control and that he would have been a candidate for some kind of cardiovascular event in the not too distant future, if he hadn't already cut short his life by other means.

Adrian Cole had died of drowning, no question about that, and the pathologist was understandably vague about time of death; somewhere between midnight and 4.00 a.m. was as close as she was prepared to call it. Time of death is never that easy to pinpoint, particularly when the body has been submerged in water and the victim has taken drugs. According to the toxicology screen, which had come back nice and quick, Cole had enough alcohol, cocaine and Ketamine in his system to knock him out, but not to kill him. Cause of death had been drowning, and the injuries, the cuts and scrapes that Callie had seen on his back, had all occurred post-mortem and were likely caused by hauling him out of the pool.

Samples of dirt taken from them, as well as of the water found in his lungs, had been sent to the lab to match against those taken at the scene. It was not the pathologist's place to rule on whether a death was either accidental, suicide or homicide; that would be down to the coroner once all the facts were in and an inquest had been held. The pathologist simply reported on the physical cause of death. In Townsend's case it was asphyxiation and in Cole's, it was drowning.

There was something about the post-mortem report on Adrian Cole that was bothering Callie, but she couldn't put her finger on it, and it niggled as she ploughed her way through the seemingly unending list of home visits.

When she finally had a moment to stop and think about it properly, she realised what it was that felt wrong; it was the amount of drugs that Cole had taken. Not enough to kill, but certainly enough to impair both his judgement and, more importantly, his ability.

How on earth had he driven to Compton's Cazeley, or even managed to find it given the state he must have been in? And having got there, what exactly was he planning to do? Why go to the trouble of having a skinny dip in your ex-boss's pool? A prank? A dare? A tit-for-tat sack me and I'll urinate in your pool sort of thing? Had he planned to do just that and then disappear home before Wendlesham had his early morning swim? With just Cole knowing what he had done to get his own back?

It all seemed somehow petty and, to Callie's mind, it would have made much more sense if Cole did actually mean to kill himself, but then, to be sure of success, he should have taken a bigger dose of drugs.

Having voiced her concerns to herself, she decided she ought to let someone know. It was the coroner who would have the final word on the cause of death – accident or suicide – but she could anticipate that he would need more information if he was going to get to the bottom of this case with any degree of certainty. Of course, no one can ever really know what was going through someone's mind just before they killed themselves, or did something like this. It could have been a rather strange cry for help or a prank gone wrong, and the coroner would likely rule it as accidental rather than suicide if there was any doubt about motive, but she felt she and Mike Parton ought to do as much digging as possible to help him make the correct decision.

When Callie finally managed to get hold of Mike Parton, he wasn't sure there was anything he could do. He told her that if there were any concerns about the death it would be up to the coroner to voice them at the inquest, or to ask for further evidence beforehand, but Callie knew the inquest was unlikely to be in the next month or two, so by the time the coroner expressed a concern, it would be too late to do any further investigation. Feeling that it had to be properly checked out before that, she rang Miller to tell him of her concerns, and to her surprise he suggested they meet later for a coffee to discuss it. He clearly wanted an excuse to get out of the office on a nice sunny day.

* * *

It was nearly half past three before she managed to finish the visits and get away from her day job, so she arrived at their agreed meeting place late, to find Miller leaning back in his chair, eyes closed, soaking up the spring sunshine at a table outside The Old Custom House.

"Sorry, I got caught up." She didn't say how, hoping he would assume it was with a patient, and not because she had almost reached the café before realising that she had left the post-mortem reports on her desk, and had had to go back and fetch them, seeing as how they were her excuse for dragging him out.

He lazily opened his eyes, squinting in the harsh sunlight, and belatedly shaded them with his hand.

"Should have remembered my sunglasses." He sat upright and moved his chair round so that he wasn't looking directly into the sun.

"You could always buy a pair at one of these kiosks." She looked over at a display of garish hats, toys and bumper stickers with rude and inane slogans, and pointed at a rack of sparkly children's glasses. "I think the pink pair would suit you best."

"I'll get them so long as you promise to get the flashing bunny ears."

"Absolutely no chance." She sat in the chair opposite him and pointed to his cup, still half-full of frothy cappuccino. "Do you want another?"

"No, thanks, don't want to be buzzing for the rest of the day."

"I thought policemen thrived on a diet of caffeine, booze and cigarettes."

"Not since The Sweeney, they haven't. Well, not the caffeine, anyway."

Callie tried to catch the eye of the waiter who was far more interested in a pair of girls with dyed blond hair and crop tops.

"Excuse me?" she said firmly after a couple of failed attempts, and he finally came over to take her order.

"I'll have an Americano with cold skimmed milk on the side," she told the waiter, who grinned and nodded. He didn't need to write it down; Callie always ordered the same thing.

"Now, what did you really want to talk to me about? I know it can't be the post-mortem report on that Adrian Cole because I've seen it, and it really isn't that interesting."

"Well, that's where you are wrong, Detective Inspector Miller."

He looked at her with a degree of resignation on his face.

"Don't tell me you are going to disagree with the pathologist?"

"No, not at all, in so far as she goes, but it's more about digging into the whys and hows."

"Oh." Miller still seemed unconvinced.

"He didn't leave a suicide note, did he?"

"Not that we've found, but you know that a lot of suicides don't–"

"Of course." She interrupted impatiently. "But he also didn't take a fatal dose of drugs."

"Maybe it was a cry for help. Hoped he'd be found."

"By the man who sacked him?"

"Who knows?"

"And how did he get there?"

"By car."

"I know by car, but how did he manage to drive?" Callie thought he was being deliberately obtuse. "He would have been seriously impaired by the drugs in his system."

"Maybe he took them there?"

"Then where are the containers? He couldn't have just had the pills in his pocket, he was naked, remember?"

"He might have chucked the bottles in a hedge or something, and we just haven't found them yet."

"Or he took them earlier and someone else drove him there."

"That's ridiculous. Why would they do that? And where did they go?" Miller sighed. "Look, you know as well as I do that different people respond differently to drugs. He might have been a long-term Ketamine user and was tolerant of quite high levels."

"But there's no evidence of that." She hesitated. "We need to test the dirt in his wounds and compare it to the samples from around the pool."

"Why?"

"Because I'm not convinced it got into his wounds when he was pulled from the pool."

"But you agreed that it was post-mortem."

"Exactly. Which would mean that he drowned elsewhere and was dragged through the bushes and dumped in the pool."

He didn't seem convinced.

"The coroner will need answers to these questions as well, you know," she added, just to make sure he agreed.

"Which is why it's Mike who needs to put the request in. It's not a CID case."

She was about to object but he stopped her.

"But I take your point and I will speak to Mike and get him to do it. No, no, don't say anymore, because that's the best you are going to get, and if Mike objects to my interference, I'll say it was you who asked for the tests, so you can take the flak."

Callie knew that this was really all about money. Both the coroner's officer and Miller agreed the tests should be done, but it was a question of whose budget would be used. Both wanted it to be someone else's and she understood that, and she also knew that now she had pushed it with them both, they would sort it out between themselves. They would never hear the end of it from her, and probably not from the coroner either, if they didn't.

"Thank you, that's–" Callie stopped as Miller's phone began to ring and he hurriedly brought it out and answered it.

"DI Miller."

He stood and walked away from her as he spoke, leaving Callie to signal to the waiter for their bill. She was just paying when he came rushing back.

"That was forensics."

"I said there was something iffy about Cole's death." Callie felt ridiculously pleased that her worries had proved right.

"No, not his, not that I know about anyway. But Giles Townsend's was. C'mon. Let's go and see what they've found."

She was so surprised that he was inviting her along that she didn't move for a moment.

"You don't want to come?" He was surprised.

"Don't be silly, of course I do." She said, grabbing her bag and almost running after him.

Chapter 10

As she saw who was waiting for them in the reception area of the private laboratory which now handled all Sussex police forensic analysis work, Callie's heart sank. She should have realised that it was Bob Jeffries who had called Miller and here he was, talking to a young man in a white coat. Jeffries didn't look overly pleased to see Callie either.

"Boss, Doc." He nodded at them both.

The man in the white coat looked at Jeffries and then realised he wasn't going to be introduced.

"How do you do?" He held his hand out to Miller. "My name is Soh Ng and I am the senior technician here."

Callie and Miller shook Ng's hand and introduced themselves and he led them through to a small office where the auto-asphyxiation harness had been laid out ready on a table.

"It has been forensically processed already, photographs, fingerprints et cetera," Ng explained. "So, we can touch."

He went over to the table and once they were all gathered around, he started his demonstration.

"This harness is designed to support the user whilst he hangs from a fixed point, I understand from the photographs that in this case it was a door frame." He looked at Miller who nodded his agreement.

"That's correct."

"It has straps that go around the upper thighs and under the groin, coming up to these around the shoulders and chest. This harness will stop the user from falling to the floor."

"It looks a bit like a parachute harness," Miller commented.

"Exactly, except for this bit here." Ng indicated a leather studded strap about ten centimetres wide that hung down from the top of the harness and chain, that in turn attached to the door frame. Callie shuddered slightly as she remembered how it had looked in situ, with Giles Townsend's body hanging from it.

"This collar goes around the neck and is tightened and released like this." He demonstrated the mechanism to them.

"Doesn't look easy," Jeffries commented. "Not when you're in the moment, so to speak."

Ng looked at Jeffries and nodded.

"That is correct, which is why this harness is designed also with a quick release mechanism here." He pointed to a thin red loop of cord attached to a metal catch. "The user has this around his left wrist."

"Leaving his right hand free to…" Jeffries used a gesture which adequately conveyed what he thought the right hand would be doing.

"Indeed." Ng was completely unfazed by Jeffries. "And then, when he wants to free himself, he pulls on the cord and it releases the catch. Also, if the user loses consciousness, the weight of his arm on the cord would be enough to release it and he would be safe. It is a very clever design."

He looked at the equipment appreciatively.

"What went wrong?" Callie asked.

"Ah yes." Ng nodded and pulled the red cord. They all looked expectantly, but nothing happened. "You see here?" He pointed to the catch and they all looked closely. "It is very hard to see but it has ethyl 2-cyanoacrylate in the catch."

They all looked at him blankly.

"Superglue," he said and they understood.

* * *

Once outside the lab, they stopped to discuss the events for a moment.

"Thank you for requesting the extra tests on Adrian Cole."

Callie was pleased that Miller had found time to ask Ng for these and had even signed the forms so that payment would be from his budget despite the comment of 'One suspicious death at a time not enough for you, Doc?' from Jeffries.

"I don't want anything else to come back and bite me. Why didn't they get around to checking Townsend's contraption earlier?" Miller was incensed. "It's bloody late to be going back and investigating his death now."

"I think they may have got the equipment a bit late," Callie added tentatively. "The pathologist didn't send it over until Mike intervened."

"What? Doesn't she understand the importance of time? How many people will have been in the flat since he died?"

"Crime scene will have done a pretty thorough job before Mike Parton released the scene. You know what a petty, nit-picking arsehole he can be," Jeffries commented.

"Not as thorough as they would have done if we had known it was murder." Miller was not going to be placated that easily.

"But is it, though?" Jeffries said. "Couldn't it be suicide? I mean, what a way to go!"

Both Callie and Miller gave that some thought; much as she could see Jeffries' point of view, she didn't believe anyone would really do that. But who was she to know?

"Why would he kill himself, though?" Miller asked. "We'll have to look at possible reasons now. Damn it to hell, we are way off speed with this one."

Callie wondered if she ought to tell him the information she had heard about Townsend and the possibility of his having been referred to the bar council, but it was only gossip at this stage and Callie really didn't want to hear Jeffries' view on sexual harassment; he probably thought women should be grateful if anyone thought they were worth harassing.

As nothing had been confirmed, she felt that it was perhaps better to wait and see if she could get any definite details. Maybe Kate had heard something back from her internet trawl? Only when she had something concrete would she take it to Miller, she decided, and it wasn't hard to stick to her decision as Miller drove her back into town, because he spent the entire journey shouting orders into his hands-free mobile as he drove.

Yes, she thought, it was definitely better to wait until he had got this investigation running on the right lines before telling him the gossip. In the meantime, she would arrange to meet Kate in The Stag to see where she had got to with her search.

The question of why the young woman who worked for the law firm had been the one to find the body niggled. It seemed to support the rumours about Giles Townsend getting junior staff to his flat, and once Miller had dropped her in town and continued on his way back to the police station, Callie decided to walk past the law firm.

She was pleased to see that she had timed it right and it looked as if they were just closing for the day. She went in just as Penny, the receptionist Callie remembered had reported finding Giles Townsend's body, was switching off her computer, ready to leave.

"Glad I caught you," Callie said, not really sure what she was going to say next, and winging it, hoping she wouldn't regret not having thought it through better. "I'm Dr Hughes, with the police; do you remember seeing me at Mr Townsend's flat? The day he died?"

Penny nodded, but said nothing, Callie was going to have to try harder.

"So, how are you doing?" It was the best Callie could come up with as an opening gambit. "I just wanted to check up on you, because finding a body can be deeply distressing."

To her relief, this was enough to get Penny talking.

"It was just awful," Penny said, before looking round to make sure no one else was listening, which would have been hard as there was no one else in the room. "They don't understand round here; I should have been given a couple of weeks off, offered counselling, all that, but have they done any of it?" She didn't wait for an answer. "Have they heck as like! They don't care, that's their problem and that snotty Ms Hersham, with her 'Pull yourself together, Penny' isn't any help at all. Who does she think she is?"

Callie never got to find out who Antonia Hersham thought she was because at that moment, the lady herself came into the room.

"Still here, Penny?" she asked. "That *is* unlike you." Sarcasm dripped from her voice, but her intonation changed only slightly as she turned her attention to Callie.

"You're the police doctor, aren't you? Can I help at all?"

"No, it's okay, I just came to check on Penny. Make sure she was okay after the shock, that's all."

Antonia didn't look as though she believed it, but she could hardly challenge Callie in front of Penny, who was rapidly collecting her things together and flinging them into a capacious handbag in preparation for a hasty exit. Callie thought that strategy was probably for the best;

there was no question that Antonia Hersham was one scary lady.

"All done," Callie said and hurriedly followed Penny out onto the street, leaving the solicitor standing in the reception area, looking after her in slight bemusement. As the door closed behind them, Callie heard the locks being turned, Antonia clearly didn't want any other unannounced visitors walking in.

As Penny hurried along the road, Callie had to almost break into a run to catch up.

"Penny!" she called and the girl stopped and turned.

"Oh, hadn't you finished?"

"No, I couldn't really talk in front of your boss. Look, why don't we go for a drink?"

"I've only got a little time before fat club."

Clearly fat club was working because Penny didn't have an ounce of spare flesh on her.

"I won't take long today, but if there are any issues I can arrange for further support if you need it." Callie felt a little bit bad that she wasn't really checking on the girl, merely trying to pump her for information, but reasoned that getting her to talk about her ordeal would probably help her in the long run and she could steer Penny towards her own GP if she really felt there was a need.

They managed to find a table outside the café and ordered tea.

"No cake," Penny said when Callie offered. "I'm being weighed later and if I haven't put any on, I'll qualify to be a gold member, so I don't want to eat anything in case." She crossed her fingers.

Callie admired the girl's will power, and at least it stopped her from ordering cake as well.

"Where do you want me to start?" Penny asked once they had their cups of tea.

"How about with that morning, arriving at work?" Callie suggested, and Penny began to tell her in excruciating detail everything she had done once she arrived at the office. At this rate they wouldn't have even got to finding the body before the tea shop closed.

"Who suggested you take the papers to Mr Townsend at his flat?" Callie finally cut in, in an effort to move things forward a bit faster.

"That was Ms Hersham. She said he was working from home."

"And was that normal?" Callie asked.

"Well, I don't know about normal. I've only been in the job three weeks and it's the second time she's asked me to do that."

Callie suspected Townsend Bartlett had a similarly high turnover of staff to Townsend's old practice.

"And the first time, it was all perfectly as you would expect?"

Penny giggled and Callie smiled. The gossip had been right.

"It was so funny! I knocked on the door and he called for me to come in. Ms Hersham had given me the key in case he was in the bathroom or something, she said, and told me to leave the brief on the table by the window. Anyway, I went in and put the papers on the table and he came out of the bedroom in nothing but a little shorty robe." She laughed again. "Sorry, I know I shouldn't say seeing as he's dead, but he looked that ridiculous! He hadn't even fastened it properly so I could see his, you know, but I didn't have the nerve to tell him. I just said, 'Here's your papers, Mr Townsend' and ran."

Callie smiled encouragingly, whilst thinking some very nasty thoughts about Giles Townsend. Thank goodness Penny didn't seem to realise that his robe falling open was probably entirely intentional. Callie wondered if it was enough of a thrill for Townsend to flash the girls or if it was only a matter of time before he stepped things up and physically assaulted them. Her money was on him pouncing sooner or later, if he hadn't been stopped before he had the chance. And what about Antonia Hersham?

Why was she facilitating his sexual assaults on members of staff? Because that was exactly what she was doing, Callie had no doubt. What was in it for her?

When she had finished with Penny, and left her with a card so she could call if she wanted to talk anything over with her again, Callie looked at her watch. Perfect timing! She should just be able to pop into M&S and pick up some essential food items, like milk and cheesecake and take it home before meeting Kate.

* * *

The Stag was a mere five minutes' walk from her flat but it was the long slow climb back up to her home at the end of the evening that kept Callie fit, toned her calf muscles and made her wonder at what age you could consider yourself old enough to admit to a desire for the flatter terrain of Eastbourne or Bexhill, even if only to yourself.

For once, Callie was the first to arrive. She bought their usual round of a pint of Spitfire for Kate and a glass of Pinot Grigio with ice for herself and found a table in the garden. The evening was warm for the time of year and it was late enough for most of the hyperactive children to be safely home; in the bath, in bed, or parked in front of the television. It wasn't that Callie didn't like children; it was just that she saw quite enough of them during her working day.

The table Callie had chosen was in the shade of a budding lilac tree that they loved to sit under, even later in the year when it was fully in bloom, although it meant they had to continually pick bits of petal out of their drinks, or rather, Callie did; Kate seemed to accept them as part of the package and drank her beer, complete with flowers and the odd midge.

Once Kate had joined her, and after checking that there was no one around who could hear their conversation,

Callie quietly told Kate about her trip to the lab and how Giles Townsend's gear had been tampered with.

"Holy shit!" Kate could hardly believe it.

"And I spoke to the receptionist who found his body. And yes, she had been sent to his flat before, and he was there in a robe that conveniently fell open, just as I heard he did at the last place he worked."

"What a creep! I should imagine the list of people happy that he's dead is quite long."

"Who would top your list?" Callie asked.

"Antonia Hersham." Kate answered without hesitation. "She's a real piece of work, that one. I can imagine her killing him to get a partnership without even batting an eyelid."

"Anyone else?"

"Anyone he waggled his willy at, I suppose."

"It seems a bit excessive to kill him for flashing. What I can't understand is why don't these women report him?"

Kate smiled.

"It's quite possible that some have, but none have actually gone through with it. There are no official records of any complaints, so none could have actually reached the tribunal stage."

"They don't keep records of dropped complaints?"

"I'm sure there would be some record, but nothing that can be accessed by the public. I asked around, but everyone was very tight-lipped when I said his name, which made me think that there have been problems but they couldn't say so. I can imagine that Giles would be quick to complain about them if they gave out information, if he were alive to do so, that is. One person even asked if I wanted to make a complaint for myself or a client and seemed surprised when I said no!"

"It makes you wonder why they have all dropped their cases," Callie said.

"No prizes for guessing that, I reckon. They were almost certainly paid off, either by Giles himself or by the practice, and made to sign a non-disclosure agreement, just so they don't go telling anyone."

"Leaving other receptionists like Penny to be harassed instead." Callie felt affronted that these women had taken the easy way out. Men like Giles needed people to make a stand against them or they would never stop. Until they were stopped, that is.

Chapter 11

A gentle drizzle had started. Callie noticed the drips running down the office window with a slight smugness born from knowing that she always had an umbrella in her bag. Just in case. She went back to checking repeat prescriptions but became aware that Richard was hesitating by the office door.

"Sorry, Richard, did you want me?"

He ambled apologetically into the room, a piece of paper clutched in his hand, which he held out tentatively to her.

"I have a patient's test results here and I wondered what you thought I should do next."

Callie took the piece of paper and saw that the patient's name was Mr Herring. Swallowing her initial reaction to thrust the paper back at Richard, she took the time to look at the results. It is every health professional's greatest fear that one of their heart-sink patients, who constantly think they have a dreadful disease but who always turn out to have nothing wrong with them at all, will one day really have an illness and they will fail to spot it. It is also a well-known rule of medicine that if you do enough tests, you can guarantee one of them will throw up an abnormality, which is why you only do tests that are suggested by the symptoms rather than a more scatter-gun approach of testing for everything. Those doctors who are inexperienced or lack confidence in themselves are often prone to over-testing and it seemed to Callie as though this might have happened with Mr Herring. One of the many tests that Richard had ordered for his patient, and which none of the other doctors would have dreamed of agreeing to, had come up as abnormal.

"He has hypercalcaemia," Richard said helpfully as Callie stared at a blood test result that told her just this.

"What symptoms did you say he had?" she asked.

"Fatigue, nausea and vomiting, forgetfulness, excessive thirst, frequent urination," Richard listed. "I was thinking diabetes, but his blood sugar was within the normal range."

"What are the causes of a raised blood calcium level?" Callie asked him, not so much to test him but to remind herself. "I assume you have looked it up?"

Richard nodded. Of course he had.

"Parathyroid disease, bone cancer, chronic renal failure, sarcoidosis, hyperthyroidism–"

Richard had clearly had more than just a quick look before coming to see Callie.

"Okay, okay." She interrupted before the list got too long. "Are any of his other tests abnormal?"

They went through all the many, many tests Richard had ordered for Mr Herring.

"Phosphate, parathyroid." Callie ticked them off in her head. "Everything normal. Except the calcium level," she commented. "What's your next move, do you think?"

Richard cleared his throat, nervously.

"I was thinking an X-ray of his hands to see if there was any sign of demineralisation and a renal ultrasound to check for nephrocalcinosis. Is that what you would do?" he asked her, unsure what she would say.

"I'd suggest running the test again, first," Callie replied, managing to dredge something from her distant memory. "Plasma calcium levels can sometimes be affected by using a tourniquet when the blood is taken, so you should ask the phlebotomist not to use one this time. We can start the other investigations if it comes back raised again and I think I'd start with timed urine levels. Always start with the cheap and easy tests first and move onto the expensive ones if necessary."

Richard nodded. She knew he'd asked for some very expensive tests already, and they'd all come back normal. And he probably hadn't shown her all of them, Callie thought to herself. She also made a note to self to look up hypercalcaemia in her medical textbooks so that she was at least one step ahead of Richard if it came back raised a second time.

With a sigh, she picked up the next item from her paperwork basket and read it. It was a note telling her that Lucy Cavendish the pathologist had rung and asked her to stop interfering in cases over which she had no jurisdiction. Oh, joy.

Her anger was not so much at what the note said – she had expected Lucy to be unhappy with her for telling Mike Parton about the equipment not having been sent for tests – but more that she had left a message with one of the receptionists. Callie slammed out of her office and went into Linda's.

"Have you seen this?" She thrust the note towards the practice manager.

Linda held up a hand to stop Callie before she went into a rant.

"If you're angry about the message from that useless pathologist, I have already spoken with Karen who took the call and explained that you probably had good reason to interfere in the first place."

"I certainly did!"

Despite being reassured that Linda had already dealt with the matter, Callie wasn't prepared to let it go so easily.

"She has no right to leave messages like that with members of staff."

"No, she doesn't and if I had taken the call, I would have told her so."

"Thank you. At least you know what she's like."

"Yes, but she doesn't know that. Believe me, she was trying to make mischief. You watch yourself, Callie."

* * *

The note from Lucy and Linda's words of warning preyed on Callie's mind throughout her afternoon visits and she decided she had to do something about it or else she wouldn't be able to concentrate on evening surgery either.

As she exited the lift into the mortuary subterranean corridor, she was surprised to hear raised voices.

"Have you sent those specimens off?" She recognised the voice as Mike Parton's.

"Of course, I have," Lucy replied.

"Really?" Parton wasn't going to be fobbed off that easily. "Only the lab say they haven't received them."

They were standing outside Lucy's office and as Callie passed a storeroom door, she could see Jim studiously sorting linen and listening to every word that was being said. Callie cleared her throat and both Parton and the pathologist turned to her.

"Oh great. Come to throw your weight around as well?"

"If you mean, have I come to complain about your call to my surgery earlier? Yes," Callie said quietly. "If you have anything to say to me, kindly say it to me direct and don't leave messages with my receptionists."

"Is that all?" She turned back to Parton and called out, "Jim!"

Jim appeared from out of the linen room and hurried to the office.

"Jim, please tell this man," she clearly couldn't bring herself to say Parton's name, "that I have sent off the samples of soil, hair and water from the drowning and therefore it is the lab who must have lost them if they say they haven't got them."

Jim, ummed and aahed and looked uncomfortable.

"Or is it you?" Lucy challenged him. "Are you trying to make me look incompetent by not sending them off? I'll have you sacked if that's the case."

It was the first time Callie had ever seen Jim looking angry. He was normally such a happy, smiley person.

"I couldn't send them, because you didn't take any samples," he said with his few teeth so tightly clenched Callie worried they might crumble.

"Don't be stupid, of course I took them. It's you who are trying to stitch me up."

"You don't need someone to stitch you up!" There was no stopping Jim now. "You can fuck things up all on your own. You were so pissed the day you did his PM, I'm surprised you were able to stand." Jim turned on his heel and walked back to the linen room leaving a stunned silence behind him.

"I'm sure you don't believe that. It's more likely it was him who was drunk." Lucy laughed nervously, but neither Callie nor Parton commented. An alcohol problem would certainly explain a lot, Callie thought, not least why she seemed to disappear for long periods of time.

"Those specimens need to be taken and sent off today," Parton finally said.

"It's not your job to tell me what I need to do or when," Lucy Cavendish replied.

"It is when you are not doing your job in a timely manner and it is affecting my cases."

"Right, now you've both had your say, get the hell out of my department." Lucy turned on her heel and went into her office, slamming the door behind her.

Parton looked at Callie and raised an eyebrow. She took a deep breath and started walking back towards the lift. He followed her and they were joined by Jim, who crept out of the storeroom, obviously trying not to be heard by Lucy. They all got into the lift unnoticed.

"That's my job up the swanny then, isn't it?"

"She won't complain, she wouldn't want any attention drawn to the department if she's drinking on the job," Callie reassured him, but he didn't seem convinced by her argument.

"Can you take and send off those samples in the Cole case without her signing them off, Jim?" Parton asked.

"You think she still won't do it?" Callie asked him, but the look on Jim's face told her that he wouldn't discount that.

"I can't believe she would not do it after this." Callie was furious. All her good work getting Miller to agree to pay for the extra tests and she hadn't even taken them, let alone sent them off.

"She'll be consoling herself with a drink now. She keeps a bottle in her desk, so God knows," Jim said.

"If you take the samples," Parton said to Jim, who was looking more than a bit worried. "I'll take responsibility and let the lab know why it hasn't been signed off properly."

Jim blew his cheeks out.

"Buggers up the chain of evidence."

"I know. But you can initial them for her."

"She'll not like it."

"That's her problem." Parton was not going to shift.

"And she might not remember enough to realise it wasn't her who took them," Callie added. "After all, she seemed pretty convinced that she had done it before."

"Aye, but it's not you that has to work with the woman."

Callie could sympathise with his dilemma.

"I'll stand up for you as well if she makes a complaint. Please, Jim, I know you don't want the pathology department to get a bad name."

"It's a bit late for that," he said, giving her an almost toothless grin as the lift doors opened. "I'll tell you what, you come on down and witness me taking them, or take them yourself." He looked at Callie. "Mr Parton can witness them, with me."

That seemed an excellent compromise.

"Thank you, Jim," Callie said warmly as the lift doors opened on the ground floor, but none of them got out. Instead, they waited until the doors closed again and the lift took them back to the mortuary.

* * *

"That woman is a real piece of work," Callie said later as she and Mike Parton, holding the evidence bags of specimens tightly, walked back to the car park.

"Tell me about it." Parton smiled but he didn't look particularly happy. "I'm going to make a formal complaint about her. I've come to the conclusion that she really needs to go before she completely and irrevocably cocks something up, if she hasn't done so already."

Callie knew this would not have been an easy decision for him to make as it would effectively end the pathologist's career.

"I agree and I'll back you up, Mike."

Parton nodded his thanks and headed for his car.

Callie wondered just why Lucy Cavendish was failing to cope with her job and had turned to drink. She had seemed like such a high-flyer when she was made locum after Ian Dunbar's death.

Callie knew there had been a complaint about failure to complete paperwork in Brighton where she trained and that was why she hadn't got the job she wanted, but surely that should have been a warning to her. If alcohol was the root of her problems, then she had been given a second chance and should have grasped it and made sure she stopped, although Callie knew it wasn't always that easy. But if she had got on with the job here in Hastings, and done well, or at least well enough, she would have been made permanent and might even have been able to go back to Brighton once she had proved herself. Instead, she could only imagine that the Board would restart the search for another person to fill the post in a substantive role and Lucy would be condemned to lower-grade locum jobs forever.

Chapter 12

His Wednesday evening ritual was sacrosanct. It started with a bottle of expensive red wine in his favourite wine bar. He drank it slowly, building the anticipation of what might happen later. His little secret – the exclusive sauna he had been frequenting once a week for the last two years. It wasn't as if there were any problems at home. No, he had a satisfactory love life, but there was no doubt it was helped by his visits to a very experienced young man who did things, and let him do things, his wife would never dream of allowing. If his wife only knew what he was fantasising about when they made love, she would be horrified. He was sure that he wasn't homosexual per se, it was just that he liked variety. He loved his wife, but he desired this young man and, under the circumstances, there was no way his wife would understand. She spent every Wednesday evening with her bible study group. Not that they seemed to study the bible much, just sat around drinking coffee, eating cake and bitching about their husbands.

He was feeling tipsier than usual as he rang the bell and waited to be let into the sauna, and he almost stumbled on the stairs that led down to the changing room; he had to grab hold of the banister to steady himself. Maybe he should ration himself to just half a bottle of wine in future, but part of the attraction of the regular night out was that he acted contrary to his norm: he had too much to drink, he spent too much money, he had sex with a young man and he paid for the experience. He giggled slightly as he thought what his friends and colleagues would think if they knew. Dear, dependable, boring John. Drunkenly shagging a boy!

He took off his clothes in the changing room and exchanged them for a towelling robe. Very few of the lockers seemed to be in use. Must be a quiet night. That was good; he wouldn't have to wait long, and could maybe have longer than usual with Giorgio, who said he was Italian but definitely wasn't. His accent and looks were more North African than Roman. But first he would have a sauna, build up the anticipation and sweat out some of the alcohol that was making him feel a bit drowsy. Wouldn't do to fall asleep on the job now, would it?

Hanging up his robe, John grabbed a clean, white towel, and almost fell into the sauna, glad that there was no one in there to see him stumble. God, it was hot tonight! The sweat was pouring off him already as he put the towel on a bench and lay down. He wouldn't stay in long, it was too hot for that, but he'd rest a short while and then he would go and find Giorgio or whatever he was really called. Just a little rest until he felt better…

Chapter 13

There was a blast of Mozart's 40th in the otherwise silent office. Callie grabbed her mobile from her bag and headed out of the room, anxious to disturb her colleagues as little as possible. As she answered it, she saw that it was the coroner's officer calling.

"Hello, Mike, what can I do for you?"

There was a slight groan from Hugh Grantham and a sigh from Gauri Sinha as they guessed who was on the end of the phone and anticipated that Callie was being called to a body and would leave them having to cover all the visits. Again. Callie closed the door behind her so that she wouldn't have to listen to their complaints.

"Hello, Dr Hughes. I thought I'd let you know that the police have decided to call in a home office pathologist to redo the PM on Mr Townsend, now that it is being classed as suspicious, and The Royal Sussex are sending over one of their pathologists to do the same for Mr Cole."

"Has Lucy gone then?" Callie asked, knowing that Parton had put in a formal complaint against her.

"Yes. I believe she has tendered her resignation and that it has been accepted with immediate effect."

Callie had to admit she admired the pathologist a tiny bit for not refusing to go, which would have meant the hospital having to suspend her on full pay pending an enquiry. She could probably have spun it out for years.

"Good. Let's just hope whoever they get to replace her is better." She didn't honestly think they could be worse. "Any idea when the PMs are scheduled?"

"I understand that they are both being prioritised due to the amount of time that has passed. Professor Wadsworth will be coming over for Mr Townsend and a Dr Iqbal is on his way from Brighton as we speak."

Callie felt a little sad that her godfather, the pathologist whose sudden death had led to Lucy Cavendish's appointment, was no longer around to moan to her that 'Wally' Wadsworth took all the best cases. She still missed him terribly.

"Will Dr Iqbal be reviewing any other cases?"

"The coroner is looking back over all the inquests he has presided over during Dr Cavendish's tenure to see if the verdict was in any way contentious, but he is hopeful that there will not be many cases where he feels a review is necessary. After all, it would appear that it is only in recent weeks that things have deteriorated."

Whilst Callie conceded that Lucy had seemed quite competent when she first started – bitter and dissatisfied with her work, true, but fully functional – that still seemed a little optimistic. People don't become alcohol dependent overnight, as a rule, and Callie wondered if the reason Brighton had been so keen to second her to Hastings was because they already knew she had a problem. If so, the Board might have cause for complaint and a claim for Brighton to fund any work needed to review her work, to ensure the correct cause of death had been found.

Callie knew that it would be an absolute nightmare if there were many cases. With a large proportion of the bodies cremated, there could only be a paper review of the findings unless specimens and slides were on file, and if the bodies had been buried, exhumation was costly and distressing for the relatives. Perhaps the speed at which they were sending Dr Iqbal over indicated a degree of guilt on the Royal Sussex County Hospital's part.

"Can you send me a list of the cases the coroner is worried about?" she asked Parton, "in case any of them affect me?"

"Of course. I'll do that as soon as I have it."

* * *

There was a degree of relief that Callie was not going to disappear and leave her colleagues to cover her work, and Hugh was happy to let her take a reduced number of visits to allow her time to drop into the mortuary and introduce herself to the new locum pathologist. It was important for Callie to speak to him as she felt she might be able to help him with information on some of the cases he would need to assess, and in particular that of Adrian Cole.

As she walked along the corridor to the pathologist's office, Callie saw the mortuary technician in the prep room, sorting out some specimens.

"Hi, Jim!" she called out to him, and he gave her a grin in return.

"You heard then?"

"That Lucy has gone? Yes, Mike called me with the news." Callie went into the prep room; she wanted to get as much of the story as possible. "What exactly happened? Do you know?"

"After Mike Parton had a go, that police bloke – Miller, is it? – came in and had his say as well, saying she'd undermined his cases with her incompetence and she just stormed off. Left everything. So, she'll not know about our little subterfuge." He winked and Callie sighed with relief. It really wasn't her job to have taken the samples, and Lucy Cavendish could have caused trouble for them all.

"She didn't turn up for work the next day and meanwhile the coroner had made an official complaint.

Chief exec came down here and was having kittens." Jim had clearly loved all this drama and didn't need any encouragement. "He searched her office to look for any indication of where she might be" — Jim clearly wasn't fooled by this explanation — "and he came out with a grim expression, several files, and a bag that clinked." Jim winked.

"Oh!" Callie was surprised the outgoing pathologist was stupid enough to have left evidence of her drinking so easy to find. There would be no coming back from this now and although Callie was relieved, she also felt sad for the woman. Why had she self-destructed quite so spectacularly? Callie knew there would be no easy answer to that question, but she hoped she hadn't in any way contributed to the situation. Perhaps she should try to find out what had gone so wrong.

"Dr Iqbal arrived from Brighton this morning. You'll like him," Jim added confidently. "He's in the office now. Hopefully he hasn't found any other bottles lying around."

Callie left the technician to his work and went in search of Dr Iqbal.

* * *

A slim man, dressed in scrubs, was sitting at the desk in the office and looked up as Callie knocked on the open door.

"Yes?"

"Hello, I'm Callie Hughes, the forensic physician." Callie smiled and held out her hand. "Just thought I'd come and introduce myself, see if I could be of any help?"

The man jumped to his feet immediately and grasped her hand firmly.

"Dr Hughes! Welcome. Billy Iqbal." He gestured to the visitor's chair, quickly clearing some files from it so that she would be able to sit down. "I've heard a lot about you from Jim."

"All good, I hope? And please, call me Callie." She settled herself in the chair and took a moment to assess the man seated across the desk from her. In his mid-to-late thirties, he was clean-shaven, with an engaging smile and dark brown eyes. Callie was pleased to see slight crow's feet either side of his eyes, indicating that he smiled a lot, something that she always found attractive.

"Very. He seems quite taken with you."

Callie hoped to goodness she wasn't about to blush.

"Yes, well, I suppose I was light relief after his manager. His previous manager, I should say."

"Lucy Cavendish? I'm sure you are right."

"Did you work with her in Brighton?"

He hesitated before answering.

"I know what you are asking, but I honestly had no idea about her drinking. She was very much the high-flyer, and the reason for her leaving was given as a personality clash with the Professor. I had no reason to question that."

Callie smiled and nodded.

"Sorry. I shouldn't have put you on the spot like that."

"No, no. Not at all. It's perfectly understandable." He smiled again. It really was a lovely smile. "Can I offer you a coffee?" He indicated a high-tech device in the corner. "Wherever I go, my Nespresso goes with me."

Callie was glad of the offer and, once they had sorted out what type of coffee she would like, watched as he found pods and cups. Making coffee was apparently as much of a ritual for Billy Iqbal as making tea had been for Ian Dunbar, right down to the importance of the right cups to drink it from. Perhaps it was a pathologist thing.

Once they were settled with their coffee, Callie asked him if he had had a chance to review any of the cases.

"Not yet. I've picked out a number of cases that give me cause for concern and will be starting with them. The coroner is sending me a list as well. Are there any that you want me to look at?"

"Adrian Cole."

"Yes, of course. He's top of my list."

"I have a confession to make." Callie looked a little awkward as she explained about taking the specimens that Lucy had failed to.

"Right," Billy said decisively. "Just to be sure there can be no question about the manner in which the specimens were collected, I shall redo them and send them off today."

"I'm sorry. It was done with the best of intentions; I wouldn't dream of interfering under normal circumstances." Callie hoped he wouldn't be angry and was pleased to see nothing but a good-natured smile in his eyes.

"I quite understand. I'll just say that, under the circumstances, I want to make sure the chain of evidence was all right."

Callie liked his tactful response to Lucy's omission and her intervention.

"It's such a strange case. What's your take on it?"

"I think there's a very real possibility that he was moved after death. And not just when he was taken out of the pool. The dirt ingrained in the grazes on his back didn't look like it came from the pool surround. It's possible he pushed his way through the hedge – he certainly left blood trace on broken twigs – but I can't see why he would have earth and leaf mulch in the grazes unless he was dragged through the hedge," Callie said.

"You're thinking he died somewhere else and someone moved him to the pool to embarrass the owner, rather than Lucy's theory that he committed suicide in situ?"

"Something like that. He certainly wasn't in a fit state to move himself anywhere much once he'd taken that amount of Ketamine. I suppose he might have commando-crawled through the bushes, but then he'd have dirt on his front, not his back."

Billy rubbed his chin thoughtfully.

"At the very least, it looks like interfering with a body and could possibly be manslaughter."

"Or, if he didn't take the Ketamine knowingly, murder."

Chapter 14

Grimacing as she sipped her insipid instant coffee – such a contrast to the lovely rich brew that she had been given by Billy Iqbal – Callie toyed with the idea of borrowing some proper coffee from Hugh Grantham's private stash. She firmly believed that the senior partner must weigh his coffee tin daily, because he always seemed to know when someone had used it. Perhaps she should get a machine for herself, something like Billy's, and put it in her consulting room, but it was cluttered enough as it was. There was no way she would be able to fit one in when she couldn't even find space for all the different forms she used on a daily basis.

Maybe when they moved to the new premises. If they moved to the new premises. Having seen the plans Hugh had shown her, Callie wasn't sure that even then they would be much better off in the new surgery. There were more treatment rooms, meeting rooms and offices in the development down by the fishing huts, but the doctors' consulting rooms still looked small. With a start, she suddenly became aware that Richard was standing by the door. She wished he wouldn't creep up on her like that!

"Er, Dr Hughes? I have the follow-up results for Mr Herring." He waved a piece of paper at her and Callie sighed as she took it. From the look on his face she knew this wasn't going to be good news. And it wasn't. The new test results were no better; in fact, they were worse. There could be no doubt that Mr Herring was ill.

"Right." Callie handed the paper back to him. "I suggest you call him and ask him to come in as soon as possible. We can do a joint appointment if you like. Liaise with Linda so we can sort that."

Callie knew as soon as she had said it that she should never have used the words 'as soon as possible' in the context of Mr Herring. Sure enough, she had barely seen one patient from her evening list before reception called through to say that he was in the surgery and telling the receptionist it was an emergency. Callie sighed. It was her fault he was in a panic, so she would have to reassure him. Telling the receptionist to warn her booked patients that there was a delay, Callie joined Richard in his consulting room, where Mr Herring was surprisingly not in his usual state of agitation. Callie was used to him moaning and complaining from the moment he opened the door until it closed behind him at the end of the consultation. Instead he sat, quiet, not frightened or anxious that they had found something wrong, but with a slight look of triumph in a 'I told you I was ill' sort of way. The trouble was, Callie felt he had every right to feel like that. After all, for years he had told her and all the other doctors that he had something wrong, and now, it seemed he was right.

* * *

It was very late when Callie finally met up with Kate in The Crown, a pub which was also in All Saints Street but closer to the seafront than The Stag. It was a favourite of Kate's as it had a good range of real ales and because she loved the bar snacks. It was absolutely packed, as it was every night, but Kate had managed to get a table. From the evidence in front of her, she had already eaten a portion of chips and some sausage pieces. She was also ready for another pint.

Callie went to the bar, ordered their drinks and, realising that she was suddenly very hungry, some crudités and dip for herself, and a portion of bread and more chips to share. Having spent almost half an hour trying to get to the bottom of Mr Herring's problem and ending up authorising a battery of expensive tests that she would have to justify to Hugh, she really felt the need to treat herself. It wasn't until she had pretty much finished eating and was well into her second glass of wine that she finally relaxed and stopped worrying about having possibly missed something serious earlier.

"It does make me wonder why I ever decided to become a doctor." She crunched a carrot stick. "Mr Herring will pursue a claim against me and I'll probably end up getting struck off for negligence. I should have taken up a career where a mistake doesn't necessarily mean you end up in front of a GMC disciplinary board."

"Any job that's well paid and interesting has a similar level of accountability. Or perhaps you should become a pathologist. From what you've said about this Lucy woman, you could get away with any number of mistakes."

"Somehow, I don't think that would be a good move for me. I do actually want to help people, living people, and I like to see daylight occasionally."

Kate quickly nabbed the last chip, just in case Callie was thinking of having it.

"Have they got someone in to sort things out?" she asked, with her mouth full.

"Yes, and how I wish he was going to stay. A real breath of fresh air."

"Oh yes?" Kate was suddenly interested.

"Not like that!" Callie hesitated. "Oh, all right then, yes, a little bit like that, but also because he seems good at his job."

"Come along, come along, tell me more."

"He's about forty, good-looking and very particular about his coffee" – Callie thought for a moment – "and he has these lovely laughter lines by his eyes."

"About thirty-nine? No one says about and then a precise number like that unless they've looked up his age on the register and know exactly how old he is but don't want to come across as too keen."

"Busted," Callie admitted with a smile. Her friend knew her too well.

"Ooh er, sounds like you're smitten. What's his name?"

"Billy. Billy Iqbal."

Kate raised her eyebrows.

"Crucial question, is he married?"

"Don't know. No ring, but that isn't necessarily definitive and it doesn't matter anyway; I have taken a solemn oath not to date anyone I work with."

That silenced Kate for a moment.

"You don't work directly with him."

"Yes, I do."

"Not if you stopped your police work. Hopefully not many of your non-police patients die unexpectedly and need post-mortems."

"No, a few, of course, but–" Callie gave the proposition some serious thought. "No." She shook her head. "And I don't want to give up the police work anyway. And" – she stopped the retort on Kate's lips – "it's not up for discussion."

Kate knew her friend's tone of voice meant that much as she might like Billy Iqbal, she would not allow herself to go out with him under any circumstances. Callie could be very stubborn once she had made a decision, and when she dug her heels in, there was no shifting her.

"Are you worried about what your mother might think if you brought an Asian doctor home?"

"Of course not. She wouldn't mind a bit. My mother might be prejudiced against men with dirty fingernails–"

"Estuary accents." Kate chipped in.

"And Geordie accents."

"Ooh, I love a Geordie accent."

"Men with bottoms and women without, bad manners and beards, but," Callie finished, "she is not a racist."

"Men with bottoms?" Kate was astounded. "I like nicely rounded buttocks."

"Apparently you cannot trust a man with a bottom."

"I like beards too," Kate mused.

"I think it's safe to say that you and my mother would not agree on suitable men."

"Very safe. She will be adding lawyers to the banned list at this rate."

"Why?"

"Have you not been keeping up with the news?"

"You mean about that Ponting woman?"

"Her, Giles Townsend, Adrian Cole and now John Dixon."

"You've lost me." Callie was genuinely confused. "I know Giles Townsend was a solicitor, but Cole worked in finance and I don't know who John Dixon is." Although, as she said the name, it did ring a faint bell.

"Adrian Cole was a corporate lawyer in a finance company, and John Dixon is a member of the SRA, the Solicitors Regulation Authority, and he collapsed in a gay sauna in London last night."

"But he didn't die?"

"No, not yet anyway, although his condition is critical."

"Probably had a stroke or a heart attack or something."

"Sure, but lawyers do seem to be dropping like flies."

"Yes. Yes, they do." Callie thought for a moment. "How did it get out that this Dixon fellow collapsed in a gay sauna?"

"Someone must have tipped off the press."

"Like with Ms Ponting."

"Yes." Kate could see where she was going with this. "And Giles."

"And Mr Cole. There was even a piece in one of the Sunday papers about his boss, what's his name?" Callie clicked her fingers. "Got it! Wendlesham. There was a spread in one of the magazines with pictures of the pool and some insinuations about his working practices."

"That's right. They suggested that he bullied staff and repeated that the firm was under review by the SFO, careful to stay just on the right side of the libel laws."

"We have two dead lawyers and two, or three if you count Wendlesham, damaged ones. Or is he actually a lawyer?"

"Dunno."

"Either way, they were all found in embarrassing circumstances and with the press tipped off in each case." Seeing as Callie seemed too lost in thought to eat, Kate helped herself to the last of the crudités.

"No." Callie shook her head and Kate paused with a piece of red pepper in her hand. "No, in this day and age, collapsing in a gay sauna isn't a real embarrassment."

"It is when you are married to the daughter of a millionaire known for his homophobia."

"Really?"

Kate nodded and mentioned the name of an American entrepreneur whose rigid views on what God thought about promiscuity, abortion and homosexuality, were often quoted in newspapers who had also highlighted his financial support of groups campaigning against them. There were also rumours that he had supported direct action in some instances. Whether or not he had permission to speak or act on behalf of God was unknown.

"You can imagine what the press have made of it."

Callie let that sink in.

"Are you thinking what I'm thinking?" Kate asked her.

"I'm not a mind reader, but I'm wondering if all these incidents are connected," Callie replied. "And if they are, whether anyone else has spotted it."

"Not to mention, who's next?" Kate finished her beer and pointed to Callie's wine glass. "Same again?"

Chapter 15

Friday was the weekday morning that was allocated for Callie to do administration. Today, however, she was using the time to visit the police station under the pretext of checking stock in the treatment room in preparation for the weekend. Friday and Saturday nights were traditionally the busiest times for a police doctor, due to the raised level of alcohol consumption in the general population. A large part of her work shifts was spent taking blood samples from suspected drink or drug drivers, or dealing with prisoners with minor injuries from pub brawls and domestics.

The real reason Callie was at the police station today, however, was that she wanted a surreptitious word with Miller so that she could bring up her discussion with Kate. Was someone really trying to humiliate and kill lawyers? Or was there some other relationship between the victims? Callie was sure that they were linked in some way; in her opinion there were too many coincidences for them not to be, but she knew it would be hard to convince Miller, particularly as the latest incident was nowhere near his patch.

When Miller was running a major investigation, such as a murder enquiry, he liked to have a briefing at half past eight every morning and again at six o'clock in the evening. The first, to allocate lines of enquiry for the day, and the latter for the team to report back on their findings. With the enquiry into Giles Townsend's death under way, Callie knew his schedule and so was confident she would find him still in the incident room at nine. Hopefully the briefing would be over and everyone else would be busy following their orders for the day.

She was pleased to see she was right, although DS Bob Jeffries looked up from his screen as she passed.

"What's up, Doc?" he asked. "Been missing us?"

Callie didn't even break her stride as she walked straight to Miller's office door. She could see him at the desk, frowning slightly as he read a report. She couldn't help but notice the dark circles under his eyes and the drawn expression. She thought that he must be working too hard.

Miller looked up as Callie knocked and entered and she thought she saw a flash of irritation at being disturbed before he recovered and smiled a welcome.

"Good morning." She closed the door behind her, hoping against hope that Jeffries would take the hint and not follow her in, but as she sat down in the only visitor chair, she could see, to her dismay, that he was making his way over.

"Morning." Miller waited as she sat and composed herself. Callie had planned exactly what she was going to say as she unpacked boxes of sterile syringes and needles in the treatment room, but now that she was in front of Miller, she couldn't remember anything.

"I wanted to talk to you about Adrian Cole," she said as Jeffries came into the room, "and Giles Townsend, Diana Ponting—"

Miller made as if to interrupt, and she hurried on to stop him. "And John Dixon."

That stopped both of them in their tracks.

"Who the fuck is John Dixon?" Jeffries asked.

Callie ignored his language and instead explained about all the different lawyers and how they had died or been caught out.

"But," Miller said as soon as she had finished, "there's no connection between them."

"They were all involved in law in some way."

"Different areas of the law, and not even in the same geographical area," Miller argued as Callie knew he would; even she had to admit the connection was tenuous.

"That Townsend bastard specialised in defending the shitbags the Ponting woman tried to put away," was Jeffries' only contribution to the argument.

"Yes," Callie agreed. "But they were all lawyers and all were humiliated in some way by the incidents."

"What's humiliating about being found skinny dipping in your boss's swimming pool?" Jeffries countered. "Bit embarrassing for the boss, but not so much for Cole."

"True, but didn't Sir Geoffrey say that there had been a problem with some emails he sent? Wasn't that the reason Cole had been sacked? He said they were outrageous if I remember rightly. Can you at least find out what they were, and if Cole really did drown in the pool?"

There was a moment's silence as Miller and Jeffries exchanged looks.

"What?" Callie asked.

Miller cleared his throat.

"The new pathologist, Dr–" Miller hesitated, trying to remember the name.

"Iqbal." Callie helped out.

"Dr Iqbal, took samples of water from Cole's lungs and the lab has confirmed that he did not die in the pool."

Callie restrained herself from punching the air.

"Did he at least drown?"

"Oh yes. He did drown, most likely in the hot tub at his own home – his clothes and phone were found there."

"He was moved after death."

"We think so, but we'll know for sure later today."

"Do you think the wife moved him? To embarrass Sir Geoffrey?"

"Seems a bit weird, but possible, I suppose."

"Or it could have been a bunch of his mates. If there was a bit of a party, all drunk, and…" Jeffries tailed off, trying to work out just how drunk they would have to be for it to seem like a good idea to dump the man in his boss's pool.

"We'll be questioning his wife later, find out what did go on that night, but look…" Miller paused to choose his words carefully. "Even if someone did move him after he'd died, it's not really much of a crime."

Callie was a little hazy on the law.

"Unlawful disposal of a body?"

"There's no reason to think they were preventing legal disposal, just delaying it slightly."

"Taking the body on tour, so to speak." Jeffries chipped in. "Not to be encouraged, on the whole, but not illegal."

"What about interfering with a body?"

"Possible," Miller agreed. "But we'd have to get CPS advice, and there's the question of whether or not it's in the public interest to prosecute."

"I suggest you ask Sir Geoffrey whether or not he wants to press charges," Callie said. She couldn't believe they were just going to let this drop.

"Of course. And the coroner might want to talk to whoever moved him about interfering with the due process of an inquest."

With a sigh, Callie accepted that they were not going to take the body of Adrian Cole being moved seriously, and were, in fact, going to pass the buck to the coroner's office.

"But why put his body in the pool?"

"To embarrass Wendlesham," Miller replied, but Callie could tell he hadn't really convinced himself about this.

"Really?"

"A city fat cat, like that?" Jeffries added. "They'd be queuing up to cause trouble."

Callie thought about it.

"You don't think this could be about something like that in all these instances?" she asked. "I mean, someone wanting to damage their businesses?"

"Why the solicitor's regulatory bods, then? That's not a business."

Jeffries wasn't going to let her get away with anything, that was for sure.

"What are you going to do about all these cases?" Callie persevered.

"Ms Ponting is being investigated by the Hampshire force due to her connection to us, and they are busy going over all her recent case decisions as well," Miller explained calmly.

Callie knew there would be serious repercussions if there was any suspicion that she had not acted competently in any prosecutions. If the hospital board were worried about Lucy Cavendish's drinking having affected any of her work, and what would happen if it got out, Ms Ponting's recent and very public incident would be an even greater worry for the CPS.

"Cole almost certainly died in Kent, even if his body was found here, so Kent are in charge of that. Dixon will be under the Met if a crime has occurred," Miller continued. "Although that seems unlikely. And we have quite enough going on with Giles Townsend, we can't make someone possibly moving a body a priority."

"And how's that going?" Callie asked.

"How's what going?" Miller countered.

"The investigation into Giles Townsend's murder?"

"Or suicide," Jeffries added.

Both Callie and Miller ignored him.

"Did you see the woman in the downstairs flat when you attended the scene?" Miller asked her.

Callie thought for a moment.

"Yes, she was comforting the receptionist who found the body – what was her name, Penny? Anyway, she was making tea for everyone and handing out biscuits."

"Can you remember anything about her?"

"Who? Penny?"

"No. The woman in the downstairs flat," Miller said in an overly patient tone.

"Why don't you go and see her, if you want to know what she's like?"

"She's gone. Now think, what was she like?"

Callie thought back to the day and tried to visualise the scene.

"She seemed nice," she ventured. "Concerned. I didn't really look at her."

"No one seems to have." Miller looked disappointed, so Callie tried harder.

"She was, well, not slim," she said tactfully. "Late thirties, maybe. Longish brown hair. In a velour leisure suit thing. Where has she gone?"

Miller shrugged.

"We can't seem to find her."

"She probably didn't like the thought of him dying up above her. Can't blame her for doing a runner," Jeffries added.

"No forwarding address?" Callie asked.

Miller shook his head.

"Maybe the tabloid press hanging round asking questions made her nervous," Jeffries continued, blissfully unaware of his poor choice of words given how Townsend had been found. "Didn't want to make it too easy for them to find her new address."

"But surely you have her details? Even if she didn't own the flat, she must have had some personal checks to rent it, surely?"

"Of course," Miller said. "The agency did a credit check and took references and everything, and we're following them up. I just find it a bit strange that she packed up and left so suddenly."

Callie agreed that it did seem odd, even if Jeffries didn't, and it frustrated her that she couldn't remember more about the woman, but she had been more concerned about the body waiting for her upstairs.

"You're worried about the downstairs neighbour disappearing, but I can't interest you in my theory about the connection between all these lawyers?"

Their completely blank faces told her that she couldn't.

"But don't let that stop you from bringing more of your crackpot conspiracy theories to us, Doc. We love 'em, don't we, boss? Don't get many laughs in this job, but you're always good value."

Callie glowered at Jeffries but it didn't make the slightest difference to the grin plastered over his face, and she wasn't mollified by the slight shake of Miller's head. He might not agree with how his sergeant had put it, but he clearly wasn't impressed by her theory either.

Callie left the office with as much dignity as she could muster, but once she had calmed down, she couldn't help thinking about the disappearing woman from the downstairs flat as she returned to the surgery to collect her afternoon visit list and the notes.

Surely, if she had just decided to leave because she didn't like the idea of Townsend dying in the rooms above, she would have been quite easy to find. Even if she didn't want the press to follow her, you would have thought she would have left a forwarding address with the rental agency at the very least, with instructions to not give it out to anyone, of course. But the police should have been able to get it, shouldn't they?

All through her afternoon visits – an elderly man with heart failure, a wheelchair-bound woman with cellulitis and a joint visit with the community psychiatric nurse to an agoraphobic – Callie wondered why the police would be having difficulty tracing the missing woman, but couldn't come up with anything other than that the woman clearly did not want to be found.

A brief internet search before evening surgery had told Callie the name of the rental agency handling the flat underneath Giles Townsend's. In a short break between patients she phoned them, pretending she had a delivery for the previous tenant and needed to know where to deliver it. She wasn't surprised when they refused to give her any information or a forwarding address, particularly as she didn't know the tenant's name. The knowledge that the agency wouldn't tell her anything wasn't in itself helpful because she still didn't know if they were telling her nothing because of data protection or because they didn't actually know where their tenant had gone.

Once surgery was over, Callie had two choices: to see whether Penny remembered anything about the woman who comforted her, or to go door to door asking if any of the neighbours had any information about her. Callie checked the time. It was after six in the evening so the neighbours were likely to be home making dinner, which reminded Callie that she hadn't eaten yet. She looked out of the window. It was dark and the rain which had been threatening all day was now a steady downpour. Not the sort of evening to go door to door. So, Penny it was and she reached for her phone.

But it seemed that all Penny could remember was that the woman had been overweight and said her name was Paula, which was at least a start, although a surname would have been better.

At home later that evening, having given up trying to trace the elusive tenant, for the time being at least, Callie settled down at her laptop to see if she could find any information to support her theory that all the crimes against lawyers were connected. First, she Googled John Dixon. There were a lot of John Dixons. Fortunately, only one was married to the daughter of a hard-line American evangelist and businessman and had recently collapsed in a gay sauna. The latest news told her that he was still in intensive care with his family holding a vigil at his bedside, his father-in-law having flown in from the States to be at his daughter's side.

What Callie wouldn't give to be a fly on the wall. She could only imagine the conversations that were going on. She idly wondered if she might know anyone at the hospital so that she could get the gossip, but she couldn't think of anyone. The club where he had collapsed was pictured and there was an interview with a rather hard-faced woman who managed it. She denied all responsibility and said that clients were warned not to use the facilities if they suffered from high blood pressure or had a heart condition, and that there were prominent signs in the basement area where the hot tubs, saunas and steam rooms were located, reminding them of this. From the information available, it certainly did look like this was just an accident, a stroke or heart attack brought on by the heat.

Perhaps John Dixon wasn't part of the pattern? But he had been left in a difficult position like the others, so that even if he survived, he would have a lot of explaining to do. To his father-in-law if not his wife.

She was getting nowhere and it was still raining, so Callie called the next person on her mental to-do list – Kate.

"I'm struggling to find connections between the lawyers," she told her friend. "And it came to me that if there was a complaint against Giles, would it have gone to the SRA where John Dixon worked? Might it even have been dealt with by him?"

"Genius!" Kate promised to get onto it in the morning. "Can you get me the dates Townsend was working for that firm where your Mum's friend said he'd had to leave because of a complaint?" she continued. "I'll find out if Dixon worked there then and if he worked in complaints at the time."

Having got the dates for Kate quite easily from a news website that had helpfully listed his work history along with a lot of carefully worded intimations about how he had died, Callie felt elated. A positive result would give them their first connection, other than that all the victims were connected with the law.

Chapter 16

Armed with the news from Kate that John Dixon had worked in the ethics department of the SRA for just under two years, which might or might not have been long enough for him to have been there when the complaint against Giles was made, and that he was indeed one of those who handled complaints against solicitors, Callie had arranged to have coffee with Miller. She had no idea how Kate had managed to get the information but assumed that she had a friend who worked somewhere in the organisation. Knowing Kate, it was probably an ex-boyfriend. Kate always seemed to remain friends with her exes, with the exception of the colleague of Callie's who had turned out to be a bit of a stalker and who had only desisted when she threatened legal action against him. Callie wasn't on speaking terms with any of her exes. She didn't know what that said about either her or Kate; it was just the way it was.

Even though it was a damp Saturday morning, she knew that with an ongoing major investigation, Miller was likely to be working. There was no way she wanted to have this conversation in front of Bob Jeffries after the reception she had got the last time, so she had suggested they meet in a coffee bar by the pier. The place was closer to the police station than to Callie's flat and, despite having an umbrella, the persistent dampness in the air meant that her hair was unusually frizzy by the time she arrived. As she sat in the window, sipping her latte and waiting for Miller, she tried to flatten the frizz as best she could. She stopped as soon as she saw him hurrying along the pavement towards the café, collar turned up against the drizzle, but no umbrella to keep his head dry.

"Sorry I'm late." Miller apologised as soon as he came through the door, taking off his coat and giving it a shake before hanging it over the back of his chair. He had barely sat down when the waitress appeared to take his order of a double espresso and a pain au chocolat. He looked at her to see if she wanted to order anything more, but she shook her head.

"I've only just had breakfast," she explained.

He looked at his watch.

"It's my day off," Callie explained. "I'm allowed to have a lie-in."

"It's eleven thirty. That's not a lie-in, that's spending the day in bed." He smiled to take the sting out of his words. "Some of us have been up working since the crack of dawn. Now, what did you want to tell me?"

At that moment, the waitress returned with his coffee and pastry and Callie sat back and waited until she had gone before saying anything.

"John Dixon. Works at the Solicitors Regulation Authority investigating complaints against solicitors."

"So you said yesterday."

"And I think he worked there when a complaint was made against Giles Townsend."

Miller leant forward, interested.

"Who made the complaint?"

"Someone from the practice where he was working at the time complained that he had sexually harassed them. Tunbridge Wells Advocacy and Law, I think it was called."

Miller was looking less interested now.

"Not recently then?"

"A couple of years back, I know. But he was at it again here."

"At what?"

"Sexual harassment. That's why the receptionist, Penny, was told to deliver papers to him at home and given a key to let herself in."

He was still looking puzzled.

"It was his thing." She lowered her voice. "He'd arrange for an office junior, female, young, pretty or whatever to deliver papers to his home and would then greet the poor person dressed only in a loosely tied robe that would conveniently fall open."

Miller sighed.

"I can't believe he was that stupid or that his partner, Bartlett, let it carry on, not after−"

He looked as if he was about to say more but then shook his head.

"Anyway," he continued. "I checked with the Met. They're not treating John Dixon's collapse as anything suspicious. It seems probable that his blood pressure dropped from being in the sauna and he fainted."

Callie looked puzzled.

"What?" he asked.

"Well, if it was just a hypotensive episode, or vasovagal attack, his blood pressure would have come up as soon as he was lying on the floor. Why is he still in hospital?"

Miller shrugged and bit into his pastry, uninterested in the medical details.

"You'd have to ask his doctors. Maybe he banged his head when he fell, or had a heart attack afterwards or something."

"Mmm." Callie gave it some thought. "Was he on any medication, do you know? For his blood pressure perhaps?"

"I have no idea. Look, the only thing you need to know is that he wasn't attacked or anything. This was entirely due to natural causes."

"Yes, but you thought that about both Giles Townsend and Adrian Cole until they found other factors that changed your mind."

He couldn't argue with that. Callie desperately wanted to brush some the crumbs off his suit, but restrained herself.

"What did Cole's wife have to say about moving his body?"

"Flatly denied it," Miller replied. "Well, she would do, wouldn't she?" He took a huge bite of his pastry, and then continued with his mouth full, "CSIs say he was definitely transported in the passenger footwell of his car. There was a pool of water there and other bodily fluids."

"If she drove him there in his car, how did she get home? And I know he wasn't a very big man, but could she have moved him?"

"I don't know how big she was, but she probably had help anyway. She needed someone to drive her home as you pointed out. Tunbridge Wells are checking CCTV and ANPR cameras to see if they can trace the journey, it's probably the most exciting thing to happen there in centuries."

Callie was sure that wasn't true but she was glad they had the time, and the manpower, to investigate how Cole's body was moved.

"Why do you think she did it?"

"She admits that they were going through a rocky patch." Miller counted the points off on his fingers. "She'd filed for divorce and she had good reason to want to embarrass Wendlesham, or rather his wife."

"Oh?" Callie sat up. "What was that?"

"Cole sent a bunch of emails before he died, which the firm tried to erase but fortunately for us and unfortunately for them he had them backed them up in the Cloud."

Miller tried to look as if he knew what the Cloud was, but failed. "In the emails he confessed to shagging clients and colleagues, including juniors and, in particular, to a passionate affair with Mrs Wendlesham."

"Lady Wendlesham." Callie automatically corrected him.

"Lady Wendlesham," Miller agreed. "And that was why Sir Geoffrey came haring back home from his holiday, that and because Cole also admitted to some insider dealing, for both himself and others, and using privileged information on clients. Not only did he back-up that email, he sent copies to the Serious Fraud Office. That's going to keep them busy for years."

"And you think his wife dumped him there because of his affair with Lady Wendlesham?"

"Yes. Kent do too." Miller looked a little uncomfortable. "Our theory is that his wife found him dead when she got back from her girls' night out at about three in the morning."

It was news to Callie that Mrs Cole had been out, but she let Miller continue with his evidence-free reconstruction of the events leading up to Cole being found in the pool.

"She knew about the emails and him getting sacked but might not have read them or known the details, then when she found his phone she took the opportunity to read all the emails."

"How?"

"It was fingerprint protected, all she needed was his thumb to open the phone."

"And where was the phone found?"

"With his clothes by the hot tub at his home, it was wiped clean, so no prints on it."

"But she didn't tidy away the evidence that he died at home? Just left the clothes and phone next to the pool for the police to find a few days later?"

"Maybe she didn't think that we'd investigate it this thoroughly. Just write it off as a suicide in the pool and leave it at that."

He didn't add that it would have been if Callie hadn't asked for the further tests.

"And she dumps the body in Sir Geoffrey's pool because she wants to get back at him for driving her husband to suicide?"

"And upset Lady Wendlesham too. Yes, I know it's a little far-fetched, but if she knew there was going to be an investigation and her life was going to be hell, she might have decided to make quite sure the Wendleshams got maximum embarrassment as well."

"Surely it would be in her best interest to let Sir Geoffrey handle it all, keep her head down and keep out of it as much as possible. She might even be able to keep some of the money that way, but moving the body? That immediately puts some of the focus on her."

"She'd had a lot to drink. You can't expect people to think clearly when they're drunk."

Callie knew only too well that people didn't think clearly when they were drunk and that they often did stupid things, but that didn't stop her from thinking that Miller was trying too hard to fit the facts to his theory rather than the other way around.

"I don't see it," Callie told him. "It just seems so unlikely, and I still think she must have had help. The drunken group of mates made more sense."

He sneaked a look at his watch and quickly gulped the last of his coffee.

"Well, it's all we've got at the moment, let's wait and see if Tunbridge Wells turn up any more evidence to support it."

"Any evidence to support it would be good."

"Got to go," he explained as he jumped up, signalled to the waitress for the bill and started putting his coat on. "It's not a day off for me, after all."

"I'll get this," Callie told him and he waved a hand in thanks as he hurried out, glad to get away from her awkward questions. Callie sat there, nursing the last dregs of her coffee and pondering what she had just heard. The thought of a drunken Mrs Cole driving her husband's body around the countryside was totally absurd, but then, sometimes life *was* totally absurd.

Chapter 17

Having finished her coffee and paid the bill, Callie wandered back into the main town for her second appointment of the day. Penny Thomas had agreed to meet her for a coffee and a sandwich. Callie thought she had better start drinking decaf or she would be buzzing by the end of the day.

It was clear that Miller was not going to get involved in John Dixon's case and was desperately trying to persuade himself and his senior officers that any investigation into Adrian Cole's death should be undertaken by Kent police. Callie understood the constraints he was under with budgets and staffing, but with different police forces investigating each incident, including Hampshire police following up on Doreen Ponting and the CPS, there was a danger that no one would put the pieces together unless she did. She was sure that they did fit together, but the question was how? It was frustrating that Miller had not been able to answer her questions on John Dixon's condition. She was going to have to get that information some other way.

The café chosen by Penny Thomas had a selection of salads, sandwiches and homemade soups, which pleased both women as it meant they wouldn't be breaking too many diet rules. It looked as if Penny was still being conscientious about her fat club regimen – her figure was as slim as ever.

Once the formalities were over and Penny had assured her that she was doing fine Callie asked her about working at Townsend Bartlett.

"How long have you worked there?"

"Nigh on a month now," Penny told her.

"And did you know the person you took over from? Or why she left?"

"No. I don't know her. I don't really know anyone who has worked there." Penny thought for a while. "If you look back at the payroll..." She glanced at Callie. "I'm allowed, I sometimes have to check things on it."

Callie would not have minded if Penny had been snooping; in fact, it might have been quite useful if she had.

"And I must say I noticed that there have been quite a few people in my job in recent years. Not that it's anything unusual, I mean, receptionists often move jobs."

But Callie thought she knew exactly why they changed so often.

"Perhaps they didn't like having to go to Mr Townsend's flat?" she ventured.

"Could be," Penny said. "It was a bit weird, now you mention it, I can see some people objecting. Not that anyone would expect to find him strung up like that."

"I don't suppose you remember any of the names of people who worked there before you?" Callie asked. "From when you checked the payroll?"

Penny shook her head and then looked sheepish.

"Well, I do remember one, actually. I was at school with her, she was the year above me. Right cow, she was. At least I thought so at the time, but that was probably because she was going out with a boy I'd set my sights on. Helena Dyrda. Polish, or half-Polish, I think she was."

Callie managed to get enough details out of Penny to be fairly confident she would be able to track this Helena down. There couldn't be too many people around with a name like Helena Dyrda.

* * *

When not on call for the surgery or police, Callie liked to spend her Saturday afternoons at the gym. A workout, a Pilates class and a swim made her feel virtuous and justified a meal out with Kate, who was supposed to be her workout buddy but somehow always managed to only turn up for the swim at the end.

Over fish cakes served with salad for Callie and steak pie with mash and gravy for Kate at their favourite haunt, Porters, Callie updated her friend with her thoughts on the cases and her plans to speak to the ex-receptionist.

"Speaking of which," Kate said, "have I got news for you!" She paused for dramatic effect. "Antonia Hersham has been announced as the new partner at Townsend Bartlett."

"What? That was quick!"

"Too bloody right. Very quick to jump in, I'd say."

"And wouldn't that make it Bartlett Hersham now?"

"Yes, they might change it, but I suspect not."

"Why? Not to honour Giles Townsend, surely? A sort of a 'lest we forget' thing?" Callie couldn't see them doing that.

"Hardly. They really do want everybody to forget him and how he died. But much more importantly, to change the name might confuse customers and would also mean they'd need a complete rebrand. If they keep the name and just add Antonia as a partner instead of Giles it will be much cheaper."

"Personally, I wouldn't worry about the expense or the possibility of losing a few customers. I'd want to erase Giles from corporate memory whatever the expense."

They both thought about that for a moment, while they ate.

"Anyway, the really good bit of gossip isn't the fact that she was made partner so soon after Giles died, but that she had expected it to happen earlier." Kate looked round to check they weren't being overheard before revealing the really salacious bit of her news. "Seems she'd been screwing him almost since she started there, on a promise of a partnership, but that somehow Giles always made excuses and didn't follow through with his side of the bargain."

"Eeuw! She was sleeping with him?"

"I don't think there was much sleep involved." Kate laughed.

"Maybe she turned a blind eye to his other peccadilloes as well."

"Like flashing the receptionists when they were sent to deliver papers to his flat?"

"Exactly – she seems to have been the one who sent them. It was definitely her who sent Penny round the morning he died. Penny told me so and I couldn't understand why she would do that at the time. Now it's a lot clearer," Callie said.

"Maybe she killed him because he was delaying her becoming a partner and she wanted him found quickly by someone other than her?"

Kate seemed pleased with this theory as it was clear she didn't like Antonia Hersham.

"Now, that's slander, Ms Ward. You can't say things like that out loud without something to back it up."

"Okay, but you can say it to the hunky police detective. That's called giving him important new information and therefore it's not slandering someone."

Callie had to admit, she had a point.

"Do you really think she could have killed Giles for not making her a partner?"

"If he was standing in her way? She'd mow him down without a thought. And causing him to die during an orgasm? That sounds like just the sort of fitting retribution she would think up."

Kate was right, Callie thought, it was rather fitting.

It was only after they had finished their food and were lingering over coffee, that Callie went back to the issue of Antonia being made partner.

"Why do you think she's been made partner now? Is she sleeping with Mervyn Bartlett as well?" she asked.

"Doubt it. Not because she wouldn't, but because he hasn't got the balls to commit adultery. Not with her, anyway. No, I suspect she's bullied him into it. Said she'll go public about Giles and his 'peccadilloes', as you so quaintly put it, if he doesn't."

Callie thought about that for a moment before nodding her agreement.

"Makes sense. You know, women like that, who help men get away with sexual harassment, are as guilty as the men themselves in my book."

"I agree. In fact, in some ways they're worse. They are betraying the rest of us as well as facilitating the assault in the first place."

* * *

After a lot of research online on Sunday morning, Callie had found out that Helena Dyrda currently worked at a hairdresser's in St Leonards and, even more helpfully, she had discovered that one of her old friends from medical school, Kathryn, now worked in ICU at the hospital where John Dixon was currently a patient. The hairdressers would not be open until Monday, so London it was. Having made a few calls and ensured that Kathryn was on duty, Callie hurried across town, trying her best to keep dry. The spring sunshine of earlier in the week seemed a lifetime ago. Her raincoat and umbrella helped keep the worst of the wet from her top half, but her ankles and feet were soaking by the time she got to the station.

* * *

With her feet still damp, and clutching her dripping umbrella, it was early afternoon before Callie reached her destination. She had arranged to meet Kathryn in the coffee shop near the main entrance, and it was a relief to sit down in the warmth with a cup of coffee and a prawn salad sandwich whilst she waited. She had expected to be kept waiting a long time. On-call registrars have a lot of people calling on their time, all of them, well, most of them, more important and more urgent than Callie, so she was pleasantly surprised to see her friend striding across the main entrance atrium soon after she sat down.

"Callie!" Kathryn called out as she carried her tray over from the counter. "Good to see you, haven't changed a bit."

Kathryn hadn't changed either and seeing her made Callie remember just how much she had liked her when they were studying together. Kathryn was always supportive, never a rival; her good-natured belief that she wanted to help people and her honesty had always impressed. She was also known for being able to drink everybody under the table, even the rugby crowd, which was no mean feat and something that Callie was never likely to be able to manage. As she took a bite of her sandwich, Callie realised that she seemed to be having a lot of conversations over food recently. It seemed to make asking questions easier somehow, but even so, she knew she wasn't going to find this an easy conversation.

"So, tell me, what can I do for you?" Kathryn asked, and when Callie hesitated, she added, "Much as I am really pleased to see you and we should meet up for a drink sometime, because it would be great to keep in touch, this isn't just a friendly meeting, is it? And I could be called away at any minute." Kathryn was straight to the point as always, and Callie understood the concern that they might not have much time.

"You have a patient who was brought in having collapsed in an embarrassing place." Callie held up her hand to stop the protest that Kathryn was undoubtedly about to make. "Hear me out, I'm not looking for gossip, but this relates to a case of mine." This was stretching the point a bit, but Callie felt she was justified under the circumstances. Having glanced round to make sure no one was listening to their conversation, she continued. "I have seen several cases of people, lawyers, being targeted, through drugs or in other ways, so that they are found in extremely embarrassing circumstances, unconscious – in some instances, dead – with details and photos released to the press. I have reason to believe someone is deliberately choosing to target these people and I need to know if this fits with how your patient was found, because not only is he a lawyer, but he was also the person who dealt with a complaint against one of the other victims."

Kathryn thought for a moment before deciding that Callie's request for information was kosher.

"Okay, yes, that would fit with the circumstances around the admission of our patient, who shall remain nameless at this point." Callie felt that was a bit unnecessary, as they both knew full well who they were talking about, but she respected her friend's need for discretion. "The press had photos of him entering the establishment as well as of him being carted off in an ambulance, so either they were told he was going to be there or someone else took them and sent them in when he collapsed."

"Is there anything iffy about his collapse?" Callie asked, more in hope than in expectation.

Kathryn looked up from her bacon butty and eyed her shrewdly.

"It's funny you should say that. His blood pressure was through the floor when he was admitted, and it took a while to get it up to normal levels and stabilise it, by which time most of his organs had shut down. We're just using supportive treatment at the moment, giving everything the chance to get working again, but his kidneys are still giving cause for concern."

Callie frowned.

"Wouldn't you only get a situation like that if he had sepsis, or a massive bleed or something?"

"I have seen some elderly patients react in that way, but they usually have something else wrong with them that their body is reacting to. We have found absolutely nothing in this case."

"Did he have a history of problems with his blood pressure?"

Kathryn smiled and Callie felt she had asked the right question.

"Yes. He had a history of hypertension and had been prescribed an ACE inhibitor and a calcium channel blocker, so we checked their levels early on."

"And?"

"He'd taken a big overdose of an ACE inhibitor along with quite a bit of alcohol. All of which, of course, he denies."

"Of course." Callie's mind was buzzing. How easy it would be to slip some extra tablets to someone, in a drink, perhaps, just enough to get them to pass out in the heat of the sauna. There might not have even been any intention to kill, just make him insensible and for an ambulance to be needed. It worked, if the point was to cause maximum embarrassment rather than death. Kathryn looked down as her bleep went off, checking to see who was calling. She looked tempted to leave it.

"Dr Goodhew, Dr Goodhew!" A young man in a white coat who didn't look old enough to have left school, let alone qualified as a doctor, was hurrying across the café, giving her no chance of hiding any longer.

"Got to go," Kathryn said as she gulped the last of her coffee and held onto what was left of her sandwich, clearly meaning to eat it on her way to whatever emergency she was being called to. "Do keep in touch, Callie. It would be interesting to hear how this pans out. Maybe we can go for that drink?" And with a wave she was gone, swallowed up by the crowds that seemed to be pouring into the hospital from all directions.

Callie sat for a while longer, finishing her late lunch and thinking about the information she had been given, and also wondering if she missed the drama and urgency of working in a hospital. As she looked at the staff, hurrying this way and that, with hardly time to have an uninterrupted meal, she decided not. No, she did not miss this or the indigestion that came from never being able to sit still and finish your food.

Chapter 18

It was Monday morning and Callie was sorting through the forms relating to patients who had been seen by the out of hours service over the weekend when she came across one that made her heart sink. Mr Herring had been admitted after an episode of slurred speech and confusion. The doctor who saw him thought he might have had a stroke and sent him straight in to hospital.

Callie checked her watch. She had time to ring and get an update before morning surgery if she was lucky. Grabbing her notes for the session, she hurried down to her consulting room so that she could have peace and quiet while making the call, knowing that she could also start her prep for the morning rush while she inevitably hung on, waiting to be put through to the right person.

She was still sitting, phone tucked under her chin as she waited, when she had finished all her preparations. She was anxiously looking at the time, thinking that she was going to have to give up, when she finally reached the medical registrar who had been on call at the weekend and who had admitted Mr Herring.

"Yeah," he told her, "we did think at first that it might have been a stroke, but there were no other signs and his

CT was clear. The stroke consultant wasn't overly impressed and then his urgent bloods came back and we decided it wasn't a cardiovascular event."

"Let me guess, he was hypercalcaemic?"

"Off the scale. Highest I've ever seen, so we decided that was the cause of his symptoms."

"I've been investigating him for this problem for a while but haven't found why it's so high, as yet."

"We're going to keep him in for a few days, bed situation permitting, see if we can get to the bottom of it, but he's already improving so…"

Callie knew exactly what he was saying. If a patient with a more urgent problem needed the bed, Mr Herring would be discharged and would once more become her responsibility. It was a sad fact that hospital beds were almost always in short supply these days.

* * *

Before she left at lunchtime, Callie found time to seek out Richard and tell him about Mr Herring.

"We'll need to keep an eye on him once he's out of hospital. I've asked them to let me know if they plan to discharge him, but we all know that it can get missed."

"I know someone in the discharge team. I'll make sure she lets us know," Richard answered. At last he was proving useful!

Callie hurried out of the surgery with a handful of visits she was determined to get through as quickly as possible. Mike Parton had informed her that Giles Townsend's inquest was due to be opened that afternoon and Callie wanted to be there even though she was probably not needed. She knew the coroner had all the statements, including her own, and that he would just open the inquest and immediately adjourn the proceedings to give the police a chance to investigate it thoroughly. It was unlikely that he would take evidence or interview witnesses at this point, but she wanted to see who else turned up, if anyone.

Normally these affairs were unattended apart from an occasional local journalist, but due to the interest in the case, Callie suspected more people would be there. It would be enlightening to see who put in an appearance, and in particular, whether Mrs Townsend or anyone from the firm attended.

The inquest opening was due to happen at Muriel Matters House, the Borough Council Building on the seafront, an entirely unexceptional sixties office block abutting a fine regency crescent and neoclassical church. Hastings was rightly proud that the well-known Australian suffragette, educationalist and Labour Party candidate for the constituency in the 1920s had chosen to settle in their town; it was just a shame there wasn't a more prestigious building to name after her.

The Borough Council Building was situated just across the road from Pelham Place car park and, although it was another grey and drizzly day, and without a tourist in sight, it took Callie a little while to find a parking space.

Arriving at the main door of the building a couple of minutes before proceedings were due to start, Callie was amazed to see a group of people hanging around on the pavement outside, including what looked like several journalists. She tried to make her way to the door but was stopped by a woman Callie recognised as being from the local newspaper. Whilst she had expected a few people to be interested by the salacious aspect of the case, she hadn't expected it to be so many.

"No point hurrying, they aren't letting anyone in," the reporter told her.

"Oh." Callie wasn't quite sure what to do next.

"Did you attend the scene?" the woman asked as Callie looked round to see how best to make her escape.

"No comment."

Both she and the journalist knew she couldn't, and wouldn't, talk about the case but experience had taught Callie that it was always easiest to make yourself scarce because one of the other journalists might not be so easy to put off. Callie looked round and saw Mike Parton looking out of a window in the main reception area. He spotted her and beckoned. Callie hurried over, pushing her way through the throng of people around the door. As soon as she got there, ignoring the questions being fired at her, he opened the normally automatic door and let her in quickly, holding up a hand to stop anyone else from trying to come in.

"Gosh, I knew there would be some interest but I hadn't expected there to be quite so many people."

"We thought we'd kept it fairly quiet but someone seems to have tipped off the press and told them that there would be a statement about some kind of development today." Mike led her down the short corridor as he spoke.

"Someone from your office?"

"No." Mike's lips were set in a firm line and he was clearly not amused by the suggestion.

"And is there?" Callie asked. "Going to be a statement, I mean?"

"Not as far as either myself or the coroner are aware." He ushered her into the council meeting room that the coroner used for inquests one day a week. A list by the door informed her of two inquests that were due to be heard later in the day, neither of them Giles Townsend's, as the coroner only wanted to open and adjourn at this point and the business would be dealt with before the other events. The room was laid out with several rows of chairs for the public placed in a semicircle in front of a long table. There were three chairs behind the table, for the coroner, the coroner's officer and the coroner's assistant, who was also the inquest manager. A chair was placed in front and to the side of the table for the person giving evidence. Mrs Townsend, dressed in an unfashionable and well-worn but useful black two-piece, was already sitting front centre and ignoring everyone else in the room.

Antonia Hersham, in a very expensive-looking suit, and Mervyn Bartlett, looking slightly less well-turned out, were also seated at the front but a few seats to one side, leaving a gap that said a great deal about the relationship between Mrs Townsend and her husband's colleagues. DI Miller was sitting towards the back. Callie smiled and sketched a small wave towards Miller. She was surprised that they were all here and wondered if they too had been tipped off about a possible statement.

The door at the back of the room opened and the coroner entered with his assistant and sat at the long table.

"Please, settle down, everybody," he said and Callie quickly plonked herself down in a free chair.

The coroner cleared his throat.

"I don't like to have closed hearings but due to the unprecedented interest in this case and the fact that I will not be taking any evidence on this occasion, I have decided to keep the public out."

Antonia Hersham leapt to her feet.

"Can I ask if you will be making any sort of statement relating to these proceedings?"

"Ms Hersham." He looked at her with distaste and then looked directly at Mrs Townsend, pointedly directing his next remark to her. "I can assure you that the only statement I will be making is that today I opened and adjourned the inquest into your husband's death." He looked back at Antonia. "And I will be investigating exactly who told the press that I would be doing anything other than that."

He looked down at his notepad and Antonia flushed with anger.

"I can assure you that no one at Townsend Bartlett had anything to do with it."

"Then you will have nothing to worry about with my investigation, will you?"

Antonia sat down, still seething with anger at what the coroner had intimated, as he did exactly as he had said he would. He declared the inquest open and then adjourned for further inquiries to take place. There was a moment of awkwardness and then everyone headed for the door. In the rush to get out, Antonia managed to elbow her way next to Mrs Townsend.

"I do hope you don't think anyone from the office would have said anything to the press?"

"No, of course not," Mrs Townsend replied, to Antonia's evident relief, before continuing, "You and the firm will have been every bit as embarrassed by this furore as me." And the older woman marched away, leaving Antonia tight-lipped with fury, again.

Back at the reception desk, Callie could see that the press pack was still waiting outside for the expected statement. There was a flash as a photographer started taking pictures through the glass and she was relieved when Parton took charge.

"The back entrance is this way," he said and led them through to the staff car park, where there was a gate out onto Castle Gardens. There was no one about, although if the press had any sense they would be hurrying round as quickly as they could run. "Mrs Townsend? Where are you parked?"

Parton had gone straight to his car and was unlocking it as he spoke.

"Pelham Place," Mrs Townsend answered quickly, getting into the passenger seat as she spoke.

"Callie!" Miller called as he too unlocked his car, but Callie just waved at him and moved towards Parton's car.

"Me too," Callie added and climbed into the back seat. Miller looked surprised and a little bit put out, which pleased Callie.

Parton started the car and was pulling away before Antonia Hersham and her sidekick, as Callie was beginning to think of Mervyn Bartlett, could ask to get in as well.

Callie resisted the urge to wave as Parton drove the car past the two of them, Antonia looking daggers at them and holding a file over her head as it started to rain. Miller was still looking puzzled but shrugged as he got into his car. He clearly wasn't going to offer a lift to the lawyers.

"I'll take you the long way around," Parton said as he indicated right at the end of the road, just as one or two of the journalists and photographers hurried up the steps towards the entrance to Castle Gardens. "If you don't mind?"

Neither Callie nor Mrs Townsend had any objection to going the scenic route to avoid the press. Both were more than happy to leave the two solicitors to answer any questions they might have.

Once they were on their way up the West Hill, Callie turned to Mrs Townsend and asked, "Did anyone contact you about the inquest today?"

"Mr Parton, of course," Mrs Townsend replied.

"But I suggested that you should not attend, Mrs Townsend, in case there were press present."

"But then I got a second call, from a girl at your office, telling me that the coroner was going to make a statement and would like me to be there."

"You mean the coroner's office?"

Mrs Townsend thought for a moment.

"No, she said she was ringing for you as you were out of the office, and that you had asked her to call and let me know."

Parton gave Callie a look in the rear-view mirror. They both knew that he had no help in the office where he was based at the police station, and there was no one that he could ask to make calls for him. The coroner's administrative office was not based in either the council or the police station, which made communication a bit laborious at times but was important in order to show that the coroner was impartial and separate from both.

Callie wondered who could have called Mrs Townsend, and presumably the press, bringing them together like that. It would be good to know if Giles Townsend's colleagues had been similarly contacted. It seemed that whoever was killing and humiliating the lawyers was set on doing the same to their family and colleagues.

* * *

Callie had barely got into the main surgery office when Richard came over to her and hovered expectantly. Callie ignored him for a moment and picked up her basket of notes before turning to him and raising an eyebrow. He really was the most exasperating young man she had ever worked with.

"Yes, Richard?" she prompted, when he didn't immediately speak.

"My friend called. From the discharge team. They sent Mr Herring home this morning."

"Already?" She put down her basket with a sigh. "I thought they would have at least kept him in a further night. I mean, they can't even have had all his results back yet." Callie knew it was pointless taking out her irritation on the messenger, and also unfair. After all, he hadn't discharged her patient, nor had he engineered the situation where there was a chronic shortage of hospital beds.

Richard stood there awkwardly for a moment, unsure what to do or say next.

"I'm sorry. I know it's not your fault. It's just frustrating when they hadn't managed to get to the bottom of his problem." She tried to think of the best way forward.

"I thought I'd visit him after evening surgery, if that's all right with you?" Richard said. Callie could have hugged him. As if it wouldn't be all right with her; what with the rush round her visits and the kerfuffle of the non-inquest, Callie hadn't even had time for a sandwich, so someone, anyone, actually volunteering to visit one of her patients was a godsend. Particularly Mr Herring.

"Thank you." It was the only response she had the energy to make as she was so tired and hungry. Linda gave her a stern look.

"Tea and chocolate biscuits required," she said. And she was right, as always.

* * *

It was only once Callie was tucked up on the sofa in her home, after an evening surgery that had seemed to last a lifetime, that she had time to think. Studiously ignoring the flashing light of the answering machine, knowing that it was almost certainly from a journalist trying to get information, she returned to her lightbulb moment from earlier and thought about the implications of both Mrs Townsend and Antonia Hersham being told that there would be some kind of statement at the inquest.

Callie would have to ask Penny if she knew anything about how the message had come in. When she thought about it, the publicity around each of the incidents looked as if they were about inflicting maximum embarrassment and getting revenge, not just on the victims, but on those around them as well. Why would anyone do that? Why would Antonia do that if she was the person who had killed Giles, now that she had her partnership? Wouldn't she want publicity around the whole affair to die down now? And why had only two of the lawyers been killed whilst others had lived to tell the tale, so to speak?

Initially, Callie had thought that perhaps it was a disgruntled client or a criminal getting revenge, but then, with the revelation that Giles Townsend was in the habit of sexually harassing his staff, Callie had begun to believe that might be the reason. Had someone's sister or daughter been a victim perhaps? But why would family and colleagues be involved? Unless, of course, it was because they allowed it to happen in some way. That seemed to make sense to Callie. Even if they hadn't actively helped, their silence might have allowed the harassment to continue. Mrs Townsend must have known about the complaint against Giles. And if she knew and did nothing, apart from hide away in her big house in the country, perhaps she could be seen as complicit in some way. And the same with the firm.

His last firm where the complaint had been made must have known at the time and, if it was still going on, Townsend Bartlett too. In fact, they must have been facilitating the abuse by sending the girls round to his flat to collect paperwork. That would make them a target, without doubt. And John Dixon might have been blamed for not following up on the complaint, perhaps. She could see how this theory worked for the Giles Townsend situation but how did Adrian Cole fit in? What had he done?

Callie took a sip of tea and thought about the possibilities. Presumably it was something related to his work, as his employer had been targeted as well. Sexual harassment again? Callie sat up, excited; she really felt she was getting somewhere. Could there have been a complaint? And could it be that the victim was the same person? It seemed a stretch. And what about Doreen Ponting? Callie couldn't believe that she was guilty of sexual harassment, although there was no reason why a woman couldn't be, but was it likely? And could it really all be related to one victim, in all these cases? It didn't seem probable, but it wasn't impossible. For someone to have been sexually assaulted or harassed at one place of work was unfortunate, but at two, or possibly three, different ones? Callie slumped back. It just wasn't feasible.

Perhaps, like John Dixon, Doreen had made the decision not to prosecute someone. That seemed a little harsh. Criminal cases had to be assessed on the likelihood of a successful prosecution. If the evidence wasn't there, and the case was unlikely to be won, she would have had no choice but to make the hard decision not to take it forward.

Much as she tried, Callie couldn't think of any other reason why these people would be targeted. But she needed to find out if there was any supporting evidence for her theory before she took it to Miller, otherwise he would just laugh at her over-active imagination. Again. However, a thought came to her that had her sitting forward in excitement. There was something that she could check that would convince him once and for all that there was a connection, and possibly even give them the name of the person who might be the suspect, or related in some way to the suspect. She just had to find a way to get the information, and she knew exactly the person who could help or, at least, point her in the right direction.

Chapter 19

As she briskly walked along the high street on her way to work, Callie sipped the double-shot espresso she had picked up from Judges Bakery. She knew it was the wrong way to try and ease her hangover; the coffee would make her more dehydrated and worsen her headache, not to mention possibly even give her palpitations to add to her problems, but she needed it. The bacon roll in her bag would help too. When she felt able to eat it. If she felt able to eat it. She had hoped the walk across the East Hill and down the steep steps leading to Tackleway and the Old Town would help clear her head, as it had on many occasions before, but it hadn't proved enough. Hence, the stop at the bakery. She took a sip of coffee and groaned quietly to herself.

The night before, in her hurry to go and see Kate, who was in The Jenny Lind Inn, Callie had forgotten that she was tired and hadn't eaten anything since the chocolate biscuits that Linda had produced for her. She was useless with alcohol at the best of times, but drinking on an empty stomach was always a bad idea. What made it worse was that Kate had been of little help and could only suggest that Callie try and see Doreen Ponting and ask her if she had ever considered a complaint against Giles Townsend, and if she had done so, whether she decided against prosecuting.

Kate had been firm; there was no way she could find out about a decision by the CPS not to prosecute someone. No one would be willing to help. She was a defence solicitor, one of the enemies, and if she tried any underhand means to get the information, she would be laying herself open to a complaint of professional misconduct. Callie would have to find the information out for herself, either through the police or from Doreen Ponting.

* * *

Having dealt with all her routine paperwork, she started trying to reach Doreen Ponting. It was unsurprising that the personal number of the head of the CPS was unlisted; after all, she wouldn't want every criminal she prosecuted leaving rude messages, so Callie had to be satisfied with leaving a message for her at the prosecution service office. She was realistic enough to figure she was hardly likely to get a response. Every journalist would be doing the same, in the hope of getting a statement, and she was sure none of the messages would be passed on. Going to her home and trying to doorstep her was unlikely to be any more productive. If she had any sense, Doreen Ponting would have gone to stay elsewhere. As far away as possible, in fact.

Anxious not to go to Miller before she had something concrete, Callie was frustrated that she seemed to be reaching a number of dead ends. There had to be a way to find out if anyone had worked at both Wendlesham's and either Townsend Bartlett or the firm in Tunbridge Wells where Giles had worked before moving to Hastings. Looking on their websites was no help, as they only listed board members or department heads and the like, and

Callie thought she was probably looking for receptionists and administrators, or possibly junior staff.

She could hardly ask the firms to send her a list of past employees, could she? She was sure they would just hide behind the data protection laws as everyone seemed to these days. If she had a name to begin with, she could try and trick them into verifying it, but she had nothing. Much as she valued her privacy, there was no doubt that current legislation didn't help her sleuthing.

She wondered if she could persuade Penny to give her a list of previous employees at Townsend Bartlett. She thought it unlikely, not to mention illegal. Meanwhile, she could try and locate Helena Dyrda, the one person that Penny had remembered having worked at the firm before her. The girl who had stolen the boy she wanted, and who now worked as a hairdresser.

* * *

Helena Dyrda, as Callie had hoped, was quite easy to find and very easy to get talking about her time at Townsend Bartlett.

"They were a weird bunch," Helena told her as she carried on cutting a middle-aged woman's hair. "I was only filling in before I got on a hairdressing course, but I was glad to leave, I can tell you."

"In what way were they weird?" Callie asked.

"Well, you know, that Mr Townsend, the one that died, he was a right pervert. I refused to take contracts round to his home for signing after the first time he flashed me, I can tell you. I mean, who wants to see something like that first thing in the morning?"

"Absolutely." Callie could tell the lady whose hair was being cut was much more interested in their conversation than the old copy of Hello magazine she was pretending to read. "Was it one of the partners who asked you to go there with the papers?"

"God no, there was only one other partner and a lady associate. The partner, Mr Bartlett, was so embarrassed when I told him what had happened, he promised he'd speak to Mr Townsend, but I don't reckon he did. He was way too scared of him."

"The lady associate then?"

"No. She was really upset about what had happened. She was the one who made me tell Mr Bartlett, but like I say, nothing happened about it and I left soon after."

Somehow, being really upset about Giles flashing didn't square with Antonia Hersham continuing to send staff to his home, but Helena had finished cutting her client's hair and was moving onto the blow dry.

"Who did ask you to go to his flat?" Callie shouted over the noise.

"Well, he did, of course. Mr Townsend."

"Not Antonia Hersham?"

"Who? No, no. It was Mr Townsend. He rang the desk and asked me to 'be a love and pop them round to him'. Ha! Never again, I can tell you!"

"Antonia wasn't the associate when you were there?"

"No, it was this other girl, really lovely, she was. Fiona, something or other. I'm terrible with names. Sorry!"

There was no point trying to continue the conversation over the roar of the hairdryer, so Callie left Helena to it and walked the short distance to Townsend Bartlett in the hope of catching Penny after work and getting more information from her about past employees.

* * *

Penny wasn't keen to talk. She told Callie that she had handed in her notice and was due to leave the firm at the end of the week. She was excited to have found a better job and was anxious about doing anything that could jeopardise her move.

"Receptionist in a beauty salon. At least I might get my nails done for free."

Callie could see the benefits of free manicures but it didn't seem like that much to risk. When asked about getting a list of past employees, Penny said, with some relief, that the moment she'd handed in her notice she'd lost her admin rights and ability to get into any of the locked files like payroll, so she couldn't help.

"Do you know how long Antonia has been with the firm?"

"About two years, why?"

It was obvious that Penny was also beginning to wonder about why Callie was asking all these questions.

"I was just trying to track down the associate before her, Fiona something or other, and wondered if you had any details?"

But Penny didn't know who she was talking about, and Callie was left wondering what on earth she could do to find out more. The name Fiona alone wasn't enough to go on, although the fact that she was an associate rather than a receptionist was interesting and Kate might be able to help track her down. At the very least, this Fiona had not approved of Giles's antics and might be willing to help Callie find others who had worked there and been sexually harassed.

* * *

Persuading Penny to talk about previous Townsend Bartlett employees was a doddle compared to trying to get more information about the possible complaint that George had talked about at her mother's dinner party all that time ago. She had even considered trying to use her mother as a go-between, but that would just open up a whole new can of worms, so she decided to go straight to see him and be upfront about why she needed to know. Even if all she got was the name of the firm involved, she might find she could persuade a receptionist or someone like Penny to help her. Unlikely as that seemed.

The crunch of her car tyres on the gravel driveway outside the converted oast house where Rita and George lived set their dog off into a paroxysm of barking. Lights were on in several rooms that Callie could see so, although there was only one car on the driveway, she was hopeful of finding them in. She hardly felt she needed to knock as the dog had quite clearly announced her presence, but she did and was rewarded, eventually, by the sound of someone coming to answer it. The door opened and a springer spaniel darted out and jumped up at her, tail wagging feverishly. Callie smiled and rubbed the dog's ears which clearly made her a friend for life. She looked up and was dismayed to see who was standing there.

"Hi Teddy," she said, with as much enthusiasm as she could muster. To be fair, he didn't look too pleased to see her either. "Are your parents in?"

"No," he said and stood there waiting for her next move, pointedly not asking her in.

"Are you expecting them back?" The spaniel was demanding more attention, so she bent and stroked her. The dog's response was to lie down and roll over, exposing her tummy, and looking hopefully at Callie who obligingly bent down, much to the animal's delight.

"Not till late." Teddy watched as Callie continued to make a fuss of the dog, if only to stop herself from having to look at the man in front of her. He was dressed in grubby joggers and a T-shirt and his bare feet revealed that he hadn't cut his toenails in quite a while. If Callie hadn't fancied him before, she certainly didn't now. "They're at a Law Society dinner," he added, "so there's no point waiting. Come in, Millie." He grabbed the dog who looked most put out at being dragged away from someone willing to give her the attention she craved, and went to close the door.

"Tell them I called by, will you?" Callie said as the door closed. She thought she heard a grunt of agreement, but that might just have been wishful thinking.

As Callie returned to her car, she wondered idly if he had a date in there, but she couldn't really imagine that he would attract anyone dressed like that. It was much more likely that he had a date with his computer.

As she drove out of the driveway, she wondered if she could get away with not dropping in at her parents, but she knew she would be bound to get caught out. Someone would have seen her distinctive car and mentioned it to her mother even if Teddy didn't pass the message on to his parents, so she drove the short distance to her childhood home and parked once again.

* * *

"No, Ma, there isn't something I'm not telling you. I just dropped by to see how you both are," Callie explained for the fifteenth time as she sat in the living room with her mother while her father washed up their dinner plates in the kitchen. Callie had never understood why they didn't get a dishwasher when she was growing up and all her friends' parents had them. But she had begun to realise that it gave her father a break. A quiet time, alone with the pots and pans. Which was why he had also refused her offer to help.

"You didn't get to eat the dinner, so you don't have to help clear up," was his firm response.

"You should have rung before coming to visit," Mrs Hughes said once they were settled with coffee. "We might have been out and then it would have been a wasted journey."

"I popped in to see Rita and George as well." That silenced her mother. Callie was pretty sure she had marked Teddy down as ineligible after the dinner party.

"You know," mused Mrs Hughes, "all that boy needs is the love of a good woman to sort him out."

Charles spluttered into his coffee as Callie considered a number of responses, from 'I'm not a good woman' to 'over my dead body'. Fortunately, she was saved from having to reply by the ring of her mobile phone. Her presence was required at the police station to assess a prisoner. Callie knew that it was most likely someone under the influence of drink or drugs, or perhaps who had managed to injure themselves before, during or even after arrest. Nothing of great interest, but at least it had cut short her visit home and stopped any further suggestion of how she might mould Teddy into marriageable material.

As she drove to the station, Callie had to concede that, on the whole, it had not been a particularly constructive day.

Chapter 20

It was not yet halfway through the week and Callie was already exhausted. The call-out to the police station had proved to be more complex than she had anticipated. A regular of hers, both as a patient and as a habitué of the custody suite, Marcy Draper, had chosen a Tuesday evening as a good time to get completely off her skull on a mixture of drink and drugs and assault one of her customers. The customer in question was in hospital having a foreign object removed from his rectum. Callie was unsurprised to find Marcy high as a kite and proud of what she had done.

"He said he wanted his money back because I hadn't done a good enough job. The fucking cheek! Snatched the cash off the fucking table and wouldn't give it back, the fucker!"

There had apparently ensued a bit of a tussle over the money, during which time the mini vibrator somehow ended up internal. Grabbing his clothes, the man had run out of the room Marcy rented by the hour and into the street. The brawl continued as Marcy attempted to get her money back and the naked man tried to get a taxi, which was never going to happen. That was when the police had got involved.

"Don't know what the fuck it had to do with them." Marcy finished her full and frank confession to Callie, who knew that it was the drugs making Marcy so honest now. Even if she allowed Marcy to be interviewed, any statement she made could and would be challenged in court. Once Callie had checked her over for injuries, of which there were many, of varying ages, but nothing requiring treatment, she told the custody sergeant they would have to let Marcy sober up and interview her in the morning.

The custody sergeant was quite happy with that; they both knew that it was unlikely that the punter would want to press charges once the vibrator had been safely removed and he understood quite how embarrassing it could be.

To make her night later still, she had run into Miller in the car park. He looked tired, exhausted even.

"We've got nothing," he said bluntly in answer to her question about how the case was going. "We can't find the woman from downstairs, she seems to have completely disappeared, everyone from the office had access to his flat because the keys were kept in an unlocked drawer. Fingerprints confirm every-bloody-one had been in the flat, including the bedroom, but only Townsend's prints are on the bondage gear."

"She can't have just disappeared," Callie said.

"Well, you bloody find her then," he answered.

"What was her name?"

"Ms Paula Davison. Her name and everything checked out. She had bank accounts and a credit history, but on doing more checking, we found that she is a long-term resident in a psychiatric facility and there's absolutely no way she could be the woman we thought she was."

"Someone stole her identity."

"But we have no idea who," he told her as he wiped his face with his hands, tiredness oozing from every pore. "I've got a press conference in the morning and nothing to tell them."

"You'd better get back and get a few hours of sleep then." Callie wasn't upset by his bad temper so much as intrigued as to how someone could steal an identity and then drop out of sight, like the woman downstairs had done. "You don't want those bags under your eyes on television."

He nodded and turned away.

"She had to have had something to do with it," Callie told his retreating back. "And she must have had a connection to the real Paula Davison."

"Presumably. But I'm buggered if I can find anything." He wandered over to his car and left Callie thinking about the news. It gave her a whole new area to investigate. Someone with a link to both Giles Townsend and Paula Davison.

* * *

Sure enough, next morning, when Callie found time to call and check on Marcy's status while taking a coffee break during surgery, she heard that she had been released and her customer had also been discharged from hospital, minus the vibrator and hopefully a wiser man.

She was exhausted after her late night and felt that she could really do with an afternoon nap. Like that was ever going to happen! The only thing to do was to keep moving, because Callie was sure that if she stopped for a moment, she would fall asleep.

First stop was the mortuary to pump Billy Iqbal for more information about the ongoing investigations under the pretext of asking after one of her other patients who had died recently.

It was gratifying to see the smile on Billy's face, and the twinkle in his eyes, when he saw who had come to visit him in his subterranean office. So few people seemed genuinely pleased to see her these days.

"And what can I do for you, Dr Hughes?" he asked, and Callie could feel a blush start at the base of her neck and run quickly up to her cheeks. She wished, just for once, she could have a conversation with a man she felt attracted to without signalling her interest to the whole world, and, more importantly, the man himself.

"Mr Candlish. I believe you did the PM this morning."

"Of course. Have a seat."

Callie sat sideways on the chair in front of his desk, the only way she could comfortably fit without first removing her kneecaps, as he brought the relevant details up on the screen of his computer.

"Ah yes, you were his GP. Well, he was generally fit for his age. No evidence of disseminated atherosclerosis. Just a major occlusion of the left anterior descending coronary artery."

"The widow maker."

Billy nodded.

"So, a heart attack, natural causes, and not something that you could have done anything about."

"Thank you. It's always nice to know you haven't missed anything. He'd certainly never complained of chest pain."

"Nice way to go, really," Billy said. "When you are in your nineties, anyway."

"Yes." Callie smiled. "Thank you for telling me."

"You know," Billy said, "you could have just waited for the report. I would have emailed it to you later this afternoon."

"That's very efficient of you."

"I'm guessing my predecessor wasn't quite so fast at getting them out."

"We were lucky if your predecessor managed to do the PMs, let alone get a report done as well."

Billy nodded again.

"I looked into it, you know."

"Into what?" Callie asked.

"Why Lucy came here." He hesitated, and Callie was pleased that he wasn't taking the issue lightly.

"According to people who knew her, she turned to alcohol after a family tragedy. Her younger sister died in an accident. The drinking began to affect her professional life and…" He shrugged.

"That's really sad. I wish I'd spoken to her, tried to help."

"I think we all wish that."

"I hope she's getting some help now."

"Yes."

They both thought for a moment, before Billy changed the subject.

"Is there anything further from the two cases the police were interested in? Giles Townsend and Adrian Cole?"

"Nothing from me. I think we are all clear on cause of death in both cases. It's down to the CSIs from this point on and I haven't heard anything more from them, or the police."

Callie tried to hide her disappointment.

"You know, I did hear on the grapevine that you like to get involved in your cases, sometimes even turn up facts previously missed or ignored by the police."

"Yes, well, sometimes the police get one possible explanation into their heads and seem to become completely blinkered to everything else."

"I know exactly what you mean. I–" He stopped as his phone started ringing. "Sorry," he said, and picked up the phone.

"Dr Iqbal."

Callie started to stand up.

"Just a moment." Billy held up his hand to stop her." "I'm just going to put you on hold for a moment," he said into the phone and pressed the button to pause the call. "Look, I'd love to continue our conversation. Discuss all the shortcomings of the local police and put the world to rights, but not at work. How about over a drink? What do you say?"

"When?"

"Tonight, if you're free?"

Callie hesitated. She didn't want to seem too keen and her liver could really do with some downtime.

"Or later in the week if that's better?" he responded to her hesitation.

"No, tonight would be fine," she said decisively.

"Excellent. You're the local, you suggest somewhere."

"How about The FILO," she said. When Billy looked confused, she added, "First In Last Out. It's on the High Street."

"Perfect." He smiled again. "Eight o'clock?"

"Perfect." Callie picked up her bag and gave a little wave as she left and he returned to his call. She almost felt like skipping as she went up the corridor to the lift and had to rapidly rearrange her face as she saw Jim looking at her from one of the autopsy suites, with a knowing smile.

* * *

"So why do you do the two jobs?" Billy asked her as they sat in The FILO later.

The evening was cool but Callie, who had been thankful that the fire in the centre of the room was lit when they first arrived, was beginning to feel a bit too warm so close to it.

"I mean, surely one career is enough for anybody." He smiled to take any sting out of his words. Not that Callie minded; it was a question she was often asked and, indeed, often asked herself.

"I could say that I feel that prisoners need someone like me to stand up for them or that the police do, but, if I'm being honest, I just like the variety. What about you? What made you get into pathology?"

Billy smiled. It was clear this was a question he was asked just as often as Callie was asked about her police work.

"I could be flippant and say I like patients that don't talk back or make complaints, but actually, it's because I find it interesting," he told her. "No! Scratch that, I don't find it interesting, I find it fascinating."

Callie smiled at his enthusiasm. It was so refreshing to meet someone genuinely happy in their work.

"I mean, sometimes you have a pretty good idea what you are going to find from the history: the enormous clot in the coronary artery like today, the bowel eaten away by a massive tumour, the multiple injuries from a car crash; but occasionally you get a real mystery that takes a lot of careful digging around before you manage to piece it all together and work out what actually killed them."

He was surprised that Callie laughed.

"I'm sorry," she said. "I just had this mental picture of you using a spade to dig around in a body and then trying to put them back together, a bit like a jigsaw puzzle."

"I haven't ever used a spade," he admitted with a grin. "Although sometimes it might be useful, but putting them back together can be very much like doing a jigsaw puzzle. Particularly when the skull has been shattered into a thousand pieces."

They drank in companionable silence for a few moments and then Callie picked up her coat and bag.

"Do you have to go?" Billy seemed surprised.

"No, not at all," she said. "It's just that I noticed that a table further from the fire just became available and you have to move fast in here."

"Phew!" Billy mopped his brow in mock relief as he collected his things together as well. "I thought it must have been something I said!"

"You don't mind, do you?" Callie nodded at the fire. "Only it was getting a bit hot."

"Of course not. I agree."

They moved over to the newly free table and Billy put his things down opposite Callie, but didn't sit.

"Would you like another drink?" he asked. "And a look at the menu? I have to admit that I'm starving."

Callie suddenly realised that she was hungry too.

"Yes, please. To both."

He gestured at her almost empty wine glass.

"Same again?"

"It must be my round." She fished in her bag for her purse.

"No. I'll get it," he said. "Consider it a bribe."

She looked at him in surprise, wondering what was going to come next.

"I want to hear all about your sleuthing when I get back."

Callie was greatly relieved, and a little disappointed, to hear that was all he was after.

* * *

"So, you haven't been able to find a link between the company where Adrian Cole worked and the company where Giles Townsend was working when he was reported for sexual harassment?" Billy asked her some time later, between mouthfuls of bubble and squeak, and ham and eggs. If Callie had been surprised by his choice from the menu, she hid it well; after all, she didn't want him to think that she had made any assumptions about him or his beliefs.

"No." Callie was busy tucking into her own plate of goat's cheese tart and salad. "Getting hold of employee records is not easy in this day and age of data protection, unfortunately."

He smiled at that.

"And getting details of the complaint to the Solicitors Regulation Authority and therefore the possible connection to John Dixon, is just as impossible because it seems to have been dropped." She looked a bit guilty.

"And I may have made out that he was definitely there when the complaint was made, but it is a bit tight. He might well have started there later and therefore have had nothing to do with it."

"But you know Townsend was still actively harassing his colleagues and employees, so there could have been more than one complaint."

"Very true, but they are not being very helpful so I'm pretty sure they wouldn't tell me even if there had." Callie thought for a moment. "It's so useful being able to discuss this with someone who doesn't just dismiss my ideas as barking mad."

"I absolutely do think they are barking mad," Billy said with a grin, "but that doesn't mean I think they are wrong."

"You mean you don't really believe that our murderer could be killing people because of historic sexual harassment?"

"It does seem a little excessive, don't you agree?"

"Killing someone is always excessive."

"True. But for this?"

"This could be a case of day in, day out, inappropriate comments, touching and pestering, even if it never goes as far as full-on assault or rape. How would you feel if it was your mother, wife, sister or daughter?" Callie didn't want to come across as some kind of harridan, and she had no idea if Billy had a sister or daughter, or, for that matter, a wife, but she genuinely thought that sometimes men just didn't get it.

Billy held up his hands in mock surrender.

"Whoa! I concede. I had never thought of it like that. You're right, it is the worst form of bullying."

"Exactly. And it can drive someone to a breakdown. Ruin their lives, their careers. I think if you were driven to despair and you saw someone getting away with it, over and over again, then you might think about killing them."

"Or if you saw a member of your family, a loved one, affected like that."

Callie had to concede he was right. It might not be the victim herself, but someone close to her. But step one was to find the person all these lawyers were connected to, and then they would be able to find the killer. And Callie had a feeling that the imposter in the downstairs flat could be both.

Chapter 21

He could feel himself sweating. He had never been good at coping with stress, and this was the most stressful situation he'd been in for years. Normally he managed to sidestep any unpleasantness or difficult jobs – that or get someone else to do it. That's how he had ended up where he was. But today, tonight, when he'd tried to ignore the email, then got caught trying to find out if the accusations were true, he'd ended up being given no choice but to be here, in Morrisons car park, as far away from the main entrance as he could get, at ten o'clock at night, to meet the blackmailers. They would find him, the email had said, and they would hand over the evidence of misappropriated funds.

In truth, it wouldn't be hard for them to find him; most of the cars had left or were leaving now that the store had closed. There were just a few remaining, huddled around the entrance, the drivers waiting to collect workers just finishing their shifts. He checked his watch; it was almost time. He looked nervously around the car park. No one else was parked in the corner where he was hiding, desperately hoping no one turned up, hoping that it was a hoax. His nerve was failing; he shouldn't be here, no good would come of meeting them. He would leave but he was scared of her, of letting her down. What she would say? Who was he more scared of? The blackmailers or her? It was hard to know.

He went to start the engine and drive away, again, but he hesitated. She would be so angry, and he couldn't stand up to her, just like he couldn't stand up to any bully, right back from when he was a schoolboy. His father had always said he should stick things out, no matter how hard it was, because it would get better once he left school. But his father had been wrong, they didn't. Things didn't change when you grew up and left school, they just changed tactics. Bullies still sought out their targets, and he was a perfect target for them. When one bully moved on, another took their place. That was the way things were and had always been.

He looked at his watch again. They were late. Perhaps they wouldn't come. He looked around and saw a car which had stopped a short distance from his. He couldn't see into the car, because of their headlights, which flashed, once, twice, the signal for the handover.

He got out and walked towards the car, quaking inside, hoping they wouldn't hurt him, and then there was a flash, and a bright light shining in his eyes. A noise, a scuffle, shouting, and he curled up in a ball, hands covering his head, a little boy again, expecting to be kicked.

Chapter 22

Next day at the surgery, it wasn't until her morning coffee break that Linda caught up with her in the kitchen and asked if she had heard.

"Heard what?"

"Clearly not if you don't know what I'm talking about."

Callie looked at her and waited. She knew that Linda was dying to tell her and didn't need prompting.

"About the chap who worked with that lawyer, the one who died when his equipment was tampered with."

"Do you mean Mervyn Bartlett?" Callie put down her cup of coffee. "What's happened to him?"

"He was targeted by one of those paedophile hunting groups. You know, the ones where a grown man pretends to be an underage girl or boy and hangs about in chatrooms hoping to tempt men into making contact."

"And Mervyn responded?"

Linda nodded.

"They said he had been grooming a child online and confronted him in Morrisons car park last night."

"How on earth do you know all this?" Callie couldn't make sense of what Linda was telling her.

"It's been reported on the local radio news and it's all on YouTube. I've just watched it."

Callie didn't know what was more surprising, that Linda knew what YouTube was or that Mervyn Bartlett was a paedophile.

"Are you sure it's him?"

"Yes."

"And does he admit it? On the video?"

"Of course not." Linda hesitated. "Actually, he seems completely gobsmacked by the accusation. But he would do, wouldn't he? After all, he was expecting to meet up with a fourteen-year-old girl, not a bunch of rugged male paedophile hunters."

Callie hurried down to her consulting room and searched on the internet for the video. It wasn't hard to find, and she sat back to watch.

The footage showed Mervyn Bartlett parking in a far corner of Morrisons car park; after a while, another car arrived and flashed its headlights. Mervyn got out of his car and looking anxiously around him walked towards the headlights. Callie had no doubt that it was him, despite the rather shaky and amateur filming. After a few moments, Mervyn's nervousness increased as a middle-aged man approached him and the person filming the meeting got closer as well. It was hard to see in the dark corners not illuminated by the camera lights, but Callie thought there were other people there as well.

"Mr Bartlett?" the first man asked him, although the sound, like the film, was of a poor quality.

Mervyn seemed to nod his head.

"Who are you?" he asked querulously and, belatedly noticing that he was being filmed, held up a hand to try and shield his face.

"We are your worst nightmare," the man said as Mervyn sobbed and covered his head with his arms, as if to defend himself from blows rather than the filming, but made no move to get away from them. The camera turned more towards the man confronting Mervyn who went on to explain for the benefit of Mervyn, and viewers, that he had been corresponding with Mr Bartlett through an internet chatroom, posing as Angel, an underage girl.

"Did you or did you not arrange to meet her here with the purpose of taking her to your home for sex, Mr Bartlett?" the man asked and Mervyn backed away from him, horror writ large across his face.

"This is madness! I never did any such thing! Go away! Go away!"

As Mervyn backed away, the man repeated his question, again and again, until Mervyn finally reached the safety of his car and jumped in, slamming the door. As he drove away, as fast as he could, his panicked face could be seen through the driver's window. Horns blared when he nearly hit a car coming into the car park in his haste. Once the car had gone the man who had approached him turned to the person with the camera.

"We shall, of course, be handing this film and all the evidence we have collected to the police." And the video ended.

Callie sat back in her chair and gave it some thought. It had never occurred to her that Mervyn could be a predatory paedophile. Had Giles sought him out because he recognised a fellow abuser? Mervyn seemed much too weak, but then, perhaps paedophiles were weak? Was that why they went for underage girls? Or, she wondered, could this be yet another event orchestrated by the killer, designed to cause maximum damage to the firm of Bartlett Townsend?

To have one pervert in a firm was unfortunate, but two smacked of institutional problems. Did the killer know Mervyn well enough to know his sexual secrets, as she had known Giles's? Well enough to exploit them, as she had done with Giles? Or had Mervyn been completely set up and was innocent, of paedophilia anyway? Either way, Miller could not any longer ignore her views that the lawyers were being targeted, whether or not they were guilty. This time, he was going to have to listen to her.

* * *

As she sat outside the café on The Stade, soaking up the lunchtime sun and watching the tourists, Callie was pleased that once again Miller had agreed to meet her away from the police station, even though she knew he must be incredibly busy. Mindful that she had visits to do before evening surgery she had already ordered herself scrambled eggs and smoked salmon, and sipped her tea as she waited for her food, and for Miller.

Despite the sunshine, the air was still cool and she was glad of her coat, but there was a real promise of spring in the air again. The prospect of spring always cheered her, and she wondered if people who lived in warm countries ever felt the joy of knowing that winter was coming to an end, even if the summer often disappointed. Perhaps they had the opposite feeling and actually looked forward to the rainy season or the cooler weather.

Miller arrived and plonked himself in the chair opposite her just as her food arrived and he looked at it hungrily as he checked his watch.

"Go on," she said. "You have to eat and service is quite quick here."

He smiled and acknowledged her point as he ordered a full breakfast, with added chips and a mug of tea to wash it down.

"Don't wait." He indicated her food and she tucked in hurriedly before it got cold and rubbery. Scrambled egg is not a dish that lasts well.

"How are things going?" Callie asked.

"I take it you've heard about Mervyn Bartlett?"

"Yes, absolutely," she said. "And seen the video. Could he have been—"

"Yes," Miller said, anticipating her question. "It's looking a distinct possibility that he was framed."

He paused as his tea arrived and the waitress set down cutlery in readiness for his food.

"Not definitely," he said quickly when he saw that Callie was about to jump in. "The techies have only had a very quick look at the account that he was apparently using to speak to this underage girl and they say he could have set up the account himself, but that it could also have been done by someone else quite easily, and there's no trace of it on any of his home or work computers, or of any other material relating to underage girls."

Miller's breakfast arrived and Callie tried not to wince as he poured rather than sprinkled salt over it.

"But supposing that this is some sort of a set-up, how did the person who did it get them all to the car park at the agreed time?"

"Oh, Mr Bartlett is quite open about that, he says he was contacted by someone who said they had information about Giles Townsend that would implicate the firm in illegal use of client funds. He was meeting them to see the evidence, or so he says."

"You think he was being blackmailed and was hoping to pay them off."

"That's definitely what Bartlett thinks was going on, anyway. He's shown us the emails. He'd rather be done for misuse of client funds than for paedophilia, although with the video all over YouTube, he's as good as been found guilty of that by the general population, anyway. Almost makes me feel sorry for the guy."

The guilt clearly didn't mean Miller had lost his appetite, Callie observed, as he shovelled the food into his mouth with alarming speed.

"So, in both cases they were called to a meeting in the car park, Mervyn to meet a blackmailer and the paedophile hunters thinking he was there to meet a young girl."

Miller nodded.

"The email account used to contact Bartlett about the blackmail was arranged in a similar way to the one that was used to access the kids' chatrooms."

Callie waited as Miller finished his breakfast.

"If Mervyn Bartlett was targeted by someone, then…?"

Miller sighed and washed his breakfast down with a large gulp of tea.

"There could be some sort of vendetta going on, yes. But" – once again, he stopped her from butting in with an 'I told you so' – "whilst there are one or two factors that also suggest Doreen Ponting was set up, they, and we, have found no links to the chap in his boss's pool or that man who collapsed in a sauna."

"But they are looking into it? I mean Adrian Cole was supposed to have sent a bunch of emails just before he died as well."

"Yes, but the tech department says that was a completely different situation, because they were definitely sent from his own account, from his phone, which was fingerprint protected."

Callie sat back, disappointed.

"And there were no emails involved with the sauna guy, and anyway, he didn't look into sexual harassment complaints. He worked strictly in financial fraud as that was his background." Miller stood and fished around in his pocket for some money. "And he wasn't even with the solicitors regulatory thingy when they investigated the complaint against Townsend when he was with that other firm in Tunbridge Wells. I can also tell you that there were no further complaints to them, so he really can't be involved, although there was—"

He was stopped from finishing his sentence by his phone ringing. He put some money on the table, answered the phone and sketched a vague wave of apology and goodbye as he walked away.

Once he had gone, Callie sat back and wondered what he had been about to say. It was gratifying that he had given credence to her conspiracy theory, at least to the point of investigating it to rule it out, and he seemed to accept that there was some kind of connection between events, if only as far as Townsend Bartlett and the CPS were concerned.

The technical department, Miller and the Hampshire police were going to be looking at how that had been organised, and by who, even if the wider conspiracy involving the other two lawyers didn't interest them and looked to be being dismissed.

Perhaps Miller was right and it was just a local thing, someone with a grudge against Townsend Bartlett and Doreen Ponting. Callie had to concede that if that was the case, then it could well be a criminal who felt he had been let down by his legal counsel and persecuted by the CPS.

With access to all the records, the police were definitely better able to investigate and find anyone who might feel that way and could have committed the crimes. But Callie was sure the other lawyers were involved in some way. And what about the woman in the downstairs flat? Paula Davison? How did she fit in? Perhaps she had got it wrong and this wasn't about sexual harassment, perhaps it was all about financial fraud. That could involve John Dixon and possibly Cole, as he was working in corporate law with a finance company.

Callie's thoughts were interrupted by her own mobile phone ringing.

"Hello," she answered it as the waitress approached with the bill. Miller had, as usual, left far too much money to cover just his breakfast. In fact, it was more than enough to cover hers as well.

Callie handed the money to the waitress and waved away the change as she listened to her call.

"Callie? It's Linda. We've had a call from Mr Herring…"

Chapter 23

Callie had been to Mr Herring's meagre, worn, but always meticulously clean and tidy flat on many occasions, but this was the first time she had been met at the door by anyone other than her patient.

"Hello dear, are you the doctor?" a frail elderly woman asked as she showed Callie into the living room. "I'm a neighbour. Gordon's in the bedroom. He's not well enough to get up, I'm afraid."

Callie followed the woman's pointed gesture towards a slightly open door and entered an oppressively warm bedroom. The pink candlewick bedspread and the faded flowers on the wallpapers and curtains suggested that this had once been a woman's bedroom – possibly Mr Herring's mother, Callie thought – and it had presumably been preserved exactly as she had left it.

Mr Herring was propped up on a large number of pale pink, frilly pillows and seemed to be asleep.

"Hello, Mr Herring, what seems to be the problem?" Callie laid her doctor's bag on the floor and sat on the edge of the bed. Mr Herring's eyes fluttered open.

"Dr Hughes. Thank you so much for coming to see me," he said weakly. "I feel absolutely terrible. Terrible."

His eyes closed again and Callie had to concede he did look pretty awful. She opened her case and got out her sphygmomanometer and stethoscope, tourniquet and blood tubes, and set about examining her patient.

"I've brought you a cup of tea, doctor," the neighbour said while Callie was listening to Mr Herring's chest.

She brought in a china cup and saucer, managing to spill most of the tea into the saucer as she searched for a space to put the cup down. Callie had to acknowledge that it was a problem, as every available surface seemed to be covered in a vast array of bottles and packets. Callie cleared a small space on the bedside table for the cup.

"Would you like a cup of tea as well, Gordon dear?" the neighbour asked Mr Herring, who raised a hand in a dismissive gesture.

"I couldn't, but thank you, Mrs Caldwell, you've been such a help," he said and flopped back against his pillows.

Once the old lady had gone again, Callie looked at the bottles that she had moved from the table to make space for the teacup. There were several different types of multi-vitamins marketed for different symptoms but all containing much the same ingredients. There were tablets marketed as being for health and vitality, to increase energy levels and combat fatigue, for the over 50s, for men, for joints, for the immune system, for the heart, for the bones. Most were well-known makes but some, Callie was dismayed to see as she moved on to look at some of the packets and bottles on the table, seemed to be from other countries, judging by the spelling of a variety of disorders they were supposed to help. Callie examined more bottles. She was beginning to get an idea of exactly what might be wrong with her patient.

"Do you take vitamin pills, Mr Herring?"

"Of course, Doctor." He seemed surprised by her question. "I do think it's the patient's responsibility to do everything in their power to keep themselves as fit and well as possible. We can't expect the NHS to look after us if we don't look after ourselves, can we?"

"No, I absolutely agree." Callie had said something very like that to many of her patients at one time or another, and it had clearly made an impression on this one; it was just a shame it was like water off a duck's back in most cases. "Perhaps we can go through these and you tell me which ones you take and how often."

Mr Herring looked at her as if she was mad.

"I take all of them, of course."

Callie sighed, reached for her bag and got out a pad of paper and a pen. She picked up the first bottle and showed it to her patient.

"I take one of those in the morning. That's what it says to do on the bottle."

Callie carefully wrote down the dosages of the various ingredients contained in one tablet and went onto the next packet.

"That's a high dose Vitamin D tablet. I read an article in a health magazine that said we don't get enough vitamin D, particularly in the winter."

Callie silenced him with a look and shook the packet.

"One a day, although since I've been unwell, I haven't been outside, so I was worried I wasn't getting enough sunlight and I've been taking two."

Callie raised an eyebrow.

"You can't buy them in health food stores because they are extra special, so you have to send for them. Over the internet," he explained.

Callie looked at the number of International Units contained in each tablet. These alone were giving him more than the recommended maximum daily allowance of vitamin D, even if he had taken only one tablet a day, but as almost all of the other multivitamins he was taking also contained smaller doses of vitamin D, he was well into toxic dose levels.

By the time Callie had been through all the supplements he was taking, she calculated that he was ingesting an average of more than ten times the daily allowance of a number of vitamins and nearer fifteen times the dose of Vitamin D. Every day.

"I think you have been taking too many vitamins, Mr Herring," Callie explained.

"But they are what keep me fit and well."

Callie avoided pointing out that he could hardly describe his current condition as fit and well.

"I know they are good for you, but only in the recommended daily dosages. Any substance can become a poison if you take too much, and you have definitely been taking too much."

Callie took a blood sample to formally confirm her diagnosis of Vitamin D poisoning and went out into the living room where the neighbour had given up pretending to clean and was openly listening.

"Do you know where I would find a plastic carrier bag?" Callie asked her. Having been pointed in the right direction, Callie took an old supermarket bag from a drawer, returned to the bedroom and loaded all the bottles of pills and potions into the carrier.

"I'm taking these with me," she told Mr Herring. "I don't want you to take anything. Absolutely no vitamin pills, do you understand?" She waited for a moment, until he reluctantly nodded his agreement. "I want you to drink plenty and eat normally if you can and, once I have your blood test result, I'll talk to the hospital to see if they think we need to admit you for a few days to make sure, or whether we can safely leave you at home to recover with the help of your neighbour."

Callie went into the kitchen and also removed a number of powders that were marketed as food supplements of one sort or another and added them to the already stuffed bag.

She returned to the bedroom and showed Mr Herring the bag.

"And no food supplements either. Let's get this lot out of your system and then I will suggest a sensible regimen for you. Okay?" Mr Herring was fortunately feeling too weak to argue, so he just nodded his head again and watched as Callie walked past Mrs Caldwell, who was unlikely to get any better entertainment today, and let herself out.

* * *

Back at the surgery, and with Mr Herring's blood samples safely on the way to the lab, Callie searched out Richard.

"I've just been to see Mr Herring," she told him, unable to disguise just how cross she was.

"I heard he'd been asking for a visit," said Richard. "I would have gone myself but I had a reflective practice session with Dr Grantham."

He clearly thought that Callie was angry because he hadn't taken the visit himself. And she was cross, as much with herself for not working it out earlier as she was with him. Although, as she pointed out to him, he had been to see Mr Herring at home so she felt he should have noticed the array of pills and potions he was taking. But mostly, she was cross with Mr Herring, for once more wasting valuable NHS time.

"Vitamin D poisoning?" Richard looked blank.

Callie shook the carrier bag at him to show him the magnitude of the problem.

"In here," she told him. "I have enough vitamin pills to kill a horse, let alone a man."

She handed the bag to Richard and he looked inside, then back at Callie, speechless with surprise.

"Amongst other things, he was taking fifteen times the daily limit of Vitamin D. I dropped an urgent blood sample off at the lab. Can you check with the on-call medical registrar and see if we need to admit him? Or can we let him detox at home now that I've confiscated his drug hoard?"

Richard merely nodded as Callie hurried off to her clinic.

Chapter 24

"I can't believe it!" Billy laughed. "He cannot seriously have taken that much Vitamin D."

"Oh, but he did. You know, it's a common belief that if a small amount of something is good for you, then a lot must be even better."

As the night was quite chill, they were sitting at a corner table in The Stag, a comfortable distance from the open fire, having a drink to unwind after their respective long days. Callie was getting a few odd looks from locals who seemed to think that she was being unfaithful to Kate by sitting at their favourite table with someone else, but Callie knew that Kate wouldn't mind. In fact, she would positively encourage her friend to have a drink with a man, and preferably do a lot more than that, although, again preferably, not in the pub.

"Yes, but this wasn't just a lot, it was bucket loads. He must have been popping pills like crazy."

Callie could see the funny side too, but for her there was also a serious lesson.

"It would have been hard for him to take a dose that high if he'd stuck to what is available and licensed for sale on the high street. The problem really began when he ordered stuff online. He was able to get a formulation that was so strong, a single tablet was an overdose."

Billy shook his head in dismay.

"There's so little regulation. Mind you, it gives me something else to check when I'm doing a post-mortem. I'll have to remember to check vitamin levels."

"And from now on, whenever I tell a patient with a poor diet that a vitamin tablet might be a good idea, I will emphasise the fact that they should only take one!"

Billy smiled and pointed to her nearly empty glass of wine.

"Wine?"

"Yes, please."

While he was at the bar, Callie marvelled at how easy conversation seemed to be with Billy. There seemed to be no side to him. He said what he meant, clearly, and didn't hint or expect her to read his mind, unlike a lot of people she knew. He had rung and asked her out for a drink. Just like that. No beating about the bush. No worrying about what people would think, how it would affect their working relationship. He said that he liked her company, and she realised she liked his, too. That didn't stop her having anxieties about going out with someone she had to work with, though. It had caused permanent damage in the past. She could never again speak directly to one consultant after a disastrous affair with him, and it would remain the case for the foreseeable future – unless he decided to leave the area and someone new, untainted by history, took over the post.

At one point, she had seriously considered leaving the area herself until Kate, dear Kate, had talked some sense into her, persuading her that it would be tantamount to running away, which was okay, and letting him win, which wasn't.

Callie put all these thoughts firmly out of her head when Billy returned with their wine. After all, he hadn't even asked her out yet, not really, just for coffee and for a drink, neither of which were Callie's idea of a proper date.

"So, have you come to any more conclusions about the lawyers?" he asked as they sipped their wine.

"Not really." Callie gave it some thought because an idea had been slowly working its way around her brain and before she knew it, she was confiding in him. "There has to be a connection and all along the police and I have had a difference of opinion on that. They seem to think that it must have something to do with a previous case and are concentrating on all the criminals that Ms Ponting has ever prosecuted and that Giles has defended, but I think it must have something to do with sexual harassment. Particularly knowing the people involved."

"But why can't you both be right?" Billy asked her. "I mean, sexual harassment *is* a crime."

"Yes, but then you would expect the police to have found a case."

"Not necessarily. We all know how hard these sorts of crimes are to prove, or even get enough evidence to bring to court. Perhaps these persons were never even charged, and your perpetrator thinks the CPS should have tried harder to do that."

"Of course! It might never have actually got to a hearing." It was such a simple and logical explanation; Callie couldn't believe she hadn't thought of it. Or that Miller hadn't either. Callie stood up.

"You are brilliant!" She gave a him a quick kiss and ran for the door, leaving him looking both pleased and more than a little bewildered.

* * *

The right house was easy to recognise from the television footage on the news and as Callie approached, slightly out of breath from the brisk walk, she was pleased to see that the press had moved on. They were no longer hanging around Doreen Ponting's home in the hope of a photograph of the fallen woman, because that was exactly the way she had been painted by the media. There was no question in any of their minds that she was some sort of a pervert and drug user. In all the news items and articles, they had left no room for discussion about the possibility of her being innocent, of having been framed. The photos showed her as drunk, drugged and in a state of undress, and even worse, in a place known for dogging. That was good enough for the press to pronounce her guilty, and it certainly sold a lot of papers.

Callie made her way towards the front door of the impressive Edwardian villa. She could see no lights on anywhere in the house and she wondered if this was just a way of stopping people from approaching the building, and the occupants, or if it really was an empty house.

Bracing herself for disappointment, she knocked at the big and imposing front door. As she had expected, there was no response. To be fair, if she were in the same position as Doreen Ponting, she wouldn't answer her door either. She rang the bell and knocked again and then shouted through the letterbox.

"It's not the press, Ms Ponting. It's Dr Hughes. Callie Hughes. I'm a forensic physician with the police. Do you remember me?" The house stayed silent. "I wanted, I really need, to discuss a theory with you. About why you might have been set up. You and others."

Callie waited with bated breath for any sign of life from inside the house and was rewarded when she felt sure she could hear the sound of someone walking quietly towards the door. The footsteps stopped and Callie started speaking again, loud enough to be heard by anyone inside, if there was anyone there.

"Ms Ponting, I'm sure you must remember me; I've been involved in a number of cases you've prosecuted. I work for the police and I promise I am not here on behalf of the press or anything. I honestly believe you are innocent and I want to discuss why this has happened to you."

There was another prolonged silence and Callie was just beginning to wonder if she had imagined the footsteps, when she heard them again, and then the scrape of the door being unbolted and unlocked before it swung open just far enough for Callie to see that it was indeed Doreen Ponting who had opened it. She stepped swiftly inside the darkened house before it was once again closed, locked and bolted securely.

"Follow me," Doreen said and Callie did, hands slightly in front of her in case there were any obstacles that she couldn't see in the dark.

There was a sudden burst of light as Doreen Ponting opened an internal door and led Callie into a warm and inviting Shaker-style kitchen. It was obviously the heart of the house, as every kitchen should be. Doreen gestured for Callie to sit at the large kitchen table.

"Coffee or something stronger?" Doreen asked her.

"Coffee. Thank you."

As Doreen filled the kettle, Callie couldn't help but notice the single dinner plate with a barely touched microwave meal for one on it, sitting next to a single wine glass and nearly empty bottle of white wine. This was a family kitchen, being used by one person. One lonely person.

"My husband is staying away for a few days. Can't say that I blame him." Doreen explained this in a voice that clearly said that she did blame him for leaving her to face the music, and the press, alone.

"Now, what is it you want to discuss, Dr Hughes?" she asked as she set down a mug of coffee and a small jug of milk in front of Callie.

"Call me Callie, please." Callie smiled and then carried on. "Has Detective Inspector Miller told you about the other lawyers who have found themselves in similar situations as yourself?"

Doreen frowned and played with her glass.

"I know about Giles of course, and I heard about Mervyn, if that's what you are referring to. I've been going through cases that I prosecuted where they were involved, but nothing seems to stand out as a reason to do this."

"Yes, but it's much more than that," Callie said and leant forward. "Adrian Cole was found floating in his employer's swimming pool, having apparently drowned there after sending self-incriminating and embarrassing emails to all of his company's clients. It was later proved that he hadn't died in the pool but had been drugged and killed elsewhere and then moved." Callie was stretching things a bit by saying he was killed rather than that he killed himself, but she needed to convince Doreen about the conspiracy.

Doreen took a tentative sip of wine, before pushing it away and going to make herself a coffee instead.

"Is he connected to this area at all?"

"Not that I know, except that Sir Geoffrey Wendlesham, the chairman and owner of the company, lives in Compton's Cazeley, so that's where the body was found, but Cole was actually killed at his home near Tunbridge Wells."

"Sir Geoffrey? That won't have pleased him. I heard he was under investigation by the SFO. The firm won't survive that." Doreen seemed to derive a certain amount of pleasure from this as she spooned instant coffee into a mug and set the kettle to boil again. "And this man was murdered, you say?"

"Probably, although it was dressed up to look like suicide." Doreen gave Callie an interrogatory look that made Callie feel immediately guilty, she certainly wouldn't like to be on the wrong end of a cross-examination by the CPS lawyer. "An overdose of drugs and alcohol in his hot tub."

Doreen raised an eyebrow.

"Were the press sent pictures and told about the emails?" she asked.

"Not in this case," Callie admitted. "There were just the emails to his clients, but the press was informed in advance in the cases of John Dixon and Mervyn Bartlett."

"John Dixon?"

"The son-in-law of–"

"Yes, yes, I know who he is, and what has recently happened to him, but what has he got to do with any of this?"

"He works for the Solicitors Regulation Authority and I wondered if perhaps he had heard a complaint against Mr Townsend or one of the others and hadn't acted on it?"

As she put her mug on the table and added milk, Doreen was not looking convinced.

"These events could just be coincidences. The law is a broad church, and you are bound to get some non-conformists amongst those working in it. These events aren't criminal. Visiting a gay sauna, practicing auto-asphyxiation, drowning in your hot tub–"

"Visiting dogging sites," Callie said, and saw Doreen's face harden. "I know you didn't go there of your own accord. What's to say someone didn't help these others on their way? Oh, I know, Giles clearly trussed himself up, but someone super-glued the release catch. John goes to gay saunas because, I don't know, maybe as a little rebellion against his father-in-law, but someone helped him collapse in there and made sure the press was around to see him carried out. Cole has a hot tub, but he hasn't drowned in one before, and are we really meant to believe that when his wife found his body, she bundled him into her car and dragged him into his boss's swimming pool simply to score a point against Sir Geoffrey? I don't believe it, not for one moment. Someone did this. Someone helped all these people, including you, to die or self-destruct, and that someone had to know you all well enough to be familiar with your personal habits."

There was a stunned silence and Callie wondered if, in her passionate defence of her theory, she had perhaps gone too far.

To her relief, Doreen finally nodded and sat down.

"How are the Hampshire police getting on with investigating your, um, predicament?" Callie didn't want to use the dogging word again, even though it had helped in convincing Doreen. She didn't want to upset the poor woman any more than was absolutely necessary.

Doreen pulled a face.

"I'm not sure they believe me." She took a sip of her coffee. "In fact, the only reason they are still trying to find someone who could have orchestrated it is the concern that all my cases might have to be re-examined. Can you believe it? All those criminals I worked so hard to send to jail, appealing against their convictions because I am now considered unreliable. The office is already swamped."

"They haven't found anything to support your story?" Callie was disheartened.

"The CCTV in the pub shows me talking to some woman and then lurching to the ladies in an intoxicated state, followed shortly after by her. The car park camera didn't cover where I was parked but the one at the entrance shows my car leaving shortly afterwards. They can't see who was driving."

"And you remember nothing?"

"No. The blood tests did show Ketamine in my system, but I was actually under the drink-drive limit for alcohol, so I can't have been staggeringly drunk as the picture seems to show."

"Which would indicate that somebody spiked your drink."

"Yes, or I took some myself, as the police seem inclined to think." She gave Callie a stern look. "I didn't though, I can assure you of that."

Callie nodded. She didn't believe the prosecutor would have knowingly taken drugs in such a public place either.

"Have the police spoken to the woman who helped you?"

"They haven't been able to find her."

"Can you describe her?"

"Well, only from the CCTV footage that they showed me. The picture was black and white and not very clear. I could see that she was overweight, taller than me, she had no problem helping me off the bar stool. Mid-length straight, darkish hair."

"And you didn't recognise her at all?"

"No, I'm sure I've never seen her before in my life."

Callie was disappointed.

"I just can't believe these incidents are coincidences. Someone, for some reason, is setting you all up."

"I am inclined to agree with you. The question is, why were these particular lawyers picked?" She put down her coffee and went out of the room, returning moments later with a laptop, legal pad and a mobile phone. Having arranged them all on the kitchen table, she switched on her laptop, picked up a pen and began making notes on the legal pad whilst the computer warmed up.

"Right. Names?" She looked enquiringly at Callie, who was slightly taken aback by this change from defeated to business-like.

"Giles Townsend and Mervyn Bartlett, obviously. Yourself, John Dixon and Adrian Cole."

Doreen wrote a name at the top of each page leaving plenty of room to add information about them.

"Dates?" She wrote the dates of each adverse event next to the names as Callie told her, along with what had happened to each of them. She then turned to the laptop and began searching for information about them in a variety of professional databases that were probably only available to members. She pushed the notepad to Callie.

"Write down the following." And she began to read out career information about everyone on the list, leaving Callie to write it all down under their names and making her feel a little bit like Doreen's personal assistant. She reminded herself that she had approached the prosecutor asking for help, so she could hardly complain and, looking at what she was writing down, Callie knew that she would never have been able to access all this information herself.

At last, Doreen stopped dictating and turned towards Callie.

"Anything interesting?" she asked.

Callie flipped between the pages.

"John Dixon wasn't at the SRA at the time of the complaints against Giles Townsend. He's only been there eighteen months or so, which agrees with what I was told by the police," Callie informed her. Doreen looked disappointed but Callie was triumphant. "But he was at Wendlesham's before that, at the same time as Cole. So, that definitely links those two cases."

They both went through all the other data, checking and rechecking dates and places, but couldn't find any further connections between all, or indeed any, of the names.

Callie leant back in her seat and threw down the pencil.

"Damn!" she said, using the worst expletive she allowed herself.

"Indeed," Doreen said. "The connection has to be someone who knew them all, rather than direct links between them."

"And what about you?" Callie asked. "Have you perhaps prosecuted someone who links these firms?"

"As I said, I have been going through all my cases for the last fifteen years, and while there are numerous people who might bear a grudge, none stand out. I think I can honestly say that I have never done any work for or against Wendlesham's; apart from anything else they are not on my patch, but I promise you, I will check. Of course, I have prosecuted many cases where either Giles or Mervyn were the defending council, but never both of them together, and anyway, none of the cases were particularly contentious. Or at least they weren't from my point of view. I just can't think why they were both targeted."

Callie sipped her coffee, although it was well and truly cold by now, and finally came to the reason why she had come to see Doreen.

"Perhaps it's not a case you prosecuted that links them. Perhaps, as you said earlier, it's a person, someone who worked for them, and who perhaps worked at Wendlesham's, someone who bears a grudge because you *didn't* prosecute one of them?"

Doreen thought for a while and sipped her own coffee before she blanched and sat forward.

"What?" Callie asked.

"There was someone," Doreen said, suddenly less sure of herself. "I declined to take forward a complaint against Giles by a member of his staff. Oh, what was her name?"

Callie held her breath.

"She was an associate, hoping to be made partner and went to the police with a complaint of rape against Giles."

"But you didn't charge him?"

"No, the story she told me was that he had pressured her into sleeping with him for the sake of her career."

"What?" Callie was angry. "He threatened to sack her if she didn't sleep with him?"

"No. Not exactly. She actually said that he promised to make her a partner if she did, but then reneged on the deal after the event, and when she complained to him about it and threatened to take action against him for rape, he told her to go ahead because she had no evidence and he in turn would make sure she never worked again."

"And you told her you wouldn't prosecute?"

Doreen Ponting rubbed a spot between her eyes. The pressure, and the wine, must have given her a headache.

"I told her to think very carefully about what she was doing. That I wouldn't be taking it forward as rape because she admitted that she had agreed to sleep with him, albeit under pressure and false pretences, but that we only had her word for that. He would and did deny it, and the jury would not look favourably on someone who, well, someone who thought she could sleep her way to the top. She wasn't helped by the fact that she was absolutely stunning. Juries are always more sympathetic towards more ordinary-looking complainants in cases like these."

She glanced apologetically at Callie.

"I know it's wrong but it's a fact of life. They would believe that she had tried to use her looks to get a partnership and was only complaining because she'd failed. There was no way a prosecution could be successful and I advised her to take it up with the SRA but that she should think carefully about it, because even if she was successful, he would probably only get a reprimand and she would be virtually unemployable as a result."

Callie was appalled.

"It's just the way the world is. She had to face up to reality."

Doreen did at least look as if she regretted the fact.

"And that's what you told her." It was a statement, not a question from Callie.

After a brief pause during which they both thought about the dire consequences that could follow sleeping with your boss, Callie asked, "Do you know what happened to her?"

"No." Doreen looked uncomfortable, aware that perhaps she should have followed it up, if not from a professional point of view then from a humanitarian one. "I would imagine she was given a handsome payoff and got herself a job elsewhere. Hopefully, she would have learnt a valuable life lesson."

Callie felt Doreen was perhaps being a little harsh on the poor woman.

"Yes, of course she should not have tried to sleep her way to the top, but she could have been put under a lot of pressure to do as he wanted. She might even have been threatened with dismissal, or a poor reference that would make moving to another job impossible. Giles was the one in a position of power, and I have absolutely no doubt that he abused that power."

Doreen had the good grace to look a little abashed.

"Yes, but it's not like she was young and inexperienced. She really ought to have known better and, as a solicitor herself, she also ought to have known that this was unlikely to lead to a successful prosecution." She sighed and then suddenly looked up. "Fiona, that was it, Fiona Hutchins – that was her name."

Callie made a note.

"When did this happen?"

"About a year ago, roughly."

"Do you know where she's working now?"

Doreen went on to the professional websites again.

"There doesn't seem to be any current position listed for her. Of course, that doesn't necessarily mean much. She's still on the register and could be freelancing. Or maybe she took her payoff and decided to take some time away from law. I can't say that I'd blame her if she did."

"Or maybe took some time off to get her revenge?" Callie suggested.

Doreen wasn't looking convinced.

"I just can't see it," she said. "The fact that she made a complaint against Giles and I declined to prosecute him doesn't tell us why she went after all the other people, does it? It's not enough to convince me. Not unless you can connect her to Wendlesham's as well."

* * *

As she walked back to her car, Callie gave that some thought. The last hour had been like being on a rollercoaster. One minute she was euphoric because they had a new connection, not to all but to some of the victims, which also matched her conviction about the motive for the crime; then, Doreen was pouring cold water on her theory, saying it was not enough. But at least they had a name. A name that she could follow up and check. Now that Mervyn had become one of the victims, he might be willing to talk to Callie about what had happened when Fiona was employed at Townsend Bartlett.

As she started the engine, she wondered if she should tell Miller. She realised that he might have been about to tell her that Fiona had made a complaint of rape against Townsend when he was called away from the coffee shop, and he would be able to check out Fiona Hutchins more easily than Callie could. But would he? Would he be convinced by this new information and act on it? Somehow Callie thought not. Miller would think, like Doreen, that it wasn't enough just yet, so perhaps it would be best if she did a little more searching for information about the woman.

If she could show that Fiona Hutchins had ever been employed by Wendlesham's, that would be her link between all the cases, and the time to tell Miller.

She had no idea how she could find that out but there were a number of places she could start. She would check the company website, and she could see if Fiona had a profile on LinkedIn with a CV listing past employers. She would get Kate to do further checks on professional websites and, even though Doreen had said Fiona Hutchins was not currently working as a lawyer, she would ask Kate to check that, because Callie had no faith that all the websites were kept rigidly up to date. She knew from checking medical ones that sometimes they were woefully behind.

Callie smiled to herself as she imagined a meeting with Miller and Jeffries where she not only handed them the details of someone with a motive for all the incidents, but also helpfully told them where they could find her.

She'd like to see the look on their faces if she did that, she thought as she drove away from Doreen Ponting's house and headed for home. She'd like to see that very much.

Chapter 25

What Callie had optimistically thought would be an easy task – finding out about Fiona and where she had worked and lived, both in the past and currently – was proving much harder than anticipated. She had spent what was left of the evening searching the Wendlesham's website, where there was no mention of a current or former employee called Fiona Hutchins.

A LinkedIn search had not come up with any suggestions at all and there were no details on the free electoral roll search for anyone with that name living in East Sussex. Of course, the details on that were probably a few years out of date too, so she had tried her name in London and was rewarded with a listing of several F Hutchins, but she had no way of knowing if any of them were the correct one, or exactly where they lived. To get more details she would need to register and she wasn't sure she wanted to do that just yet.

Callie realised that she would get much more up-to-date information if she went to the library and examined the electoral roll there. Or she could ask Kate. Callie knew that Kate had bought a disk of the local electoral roll some time before, ostensibly to check client details, but Callie suspected she also used it to look up the men she dated, making sure they didn't have other adult females listed in their household. Kate wasn't quite as concerned as Callie that her boyfriends were truly available, but she liked to know where she stood.

The information on the disk would be a few years out of date now, but probably more recent than the details freely obtainable online. She also decided to ask Kate about freelancers. She was kicking herself for not asking Doreen about them.

She also thought that Kate might know someone who knew Fiona from the time she spent at Townsend Bartlett and that she might get more information that way. Despite the late hour, thankfully, Kate was not asleep or otherwise engaged, and picked up the phone straight away.

"But I know Fiona!" Was the immediate response from Kate, surprising them both. "Or rather, I used to know her; haven't seen her in ages."

"How long ago is ages?" Callie asked. There were a few moments' silence as Kate gave that some thought.

"Must be about a year, maybe more like eighteen months. She did work at Townsend Bartlett now I come to think of it."

"And you didn't think to mention it before?" Callie asked in exasperation.

"I'd completely forgotten her."

"I thought it was more likely to be someone in a role like that, given how Giles seems to have behaved, but apparently he slept with Fiona and promised to make her a partner."

"God, sleeping with the boss. Never a good idea."

"No, as she found out to her cost." They both paused, thinking about mistakes they had each made in the past. Again.

"And you honestly think she could have something to do with this?"

"Her or someone connected to her." Callie explained about the woman who had rented the flat downstairs to Giles and the description of the woman seen helping Doreen.

"It is possible the two women were actually the same person." Callie knew she was stretching it, given that the description could fit half the women in Hastings.

"And the police have been unable to trace either of them?"

"That's right, and it does seem strange."

"That can't be Fiona though. It doesn't sound like her at all. I mean, she's absolutely gorgeous. Legs up to her armpits and glossy blonde hair. Had all the men in the Law Society meetings absolutely drooling."

"Hmm. No. That doesn't sound like our woman, but it could be someone connected with her. Do you know anything about her family? Where she's from? Anything?"

Kate thought for a moment.

"No. I can't honestly remember talking to her about personal things. I seem to remember the most we did was swap war stories about work; not that she mentioned she was sleeping with one of the partners or that he was into any interesting sexual practices. Believe me, I'd have remembered if she had."

Callie could believe it.

"What about mutual friends? Do you know anyone who might have known her better than you?"

Kate was not sure that she did.

"The trouble is, when someone is so bloody good-looking, the men are all trying to hit on her, and failing miserably, I might add, and the women are all so insanely jealous that no one actually befriends them, if you know what I mean?"

Callie did know what she meant. She remembered a particular medical student she had trained with who had always had a crowd of male admirers hanging around but was never invited to anything by the female students because of it. Callie had visited her when she was admitted to the psychiatric wing after a suicide attempt. It seems that her male admirers were only interested in one thing and were pretty hopeless when she got into difficulties with her studies and it all got too much for her. There was no one for her to turn to when she needed help and support. She went home soon after she was discharged from the unit and never did complete her studies. Callie had felt terribly guilty that she and her friends had not been there for a fellow female medic.

"I'll have a think about it and do some digging for you," Kate finished. "I'll let you know if there are any details on my electoral roll disk or if I come up with anyone or anything of interest."

Callie had to be content with that.

* * *

Later, as she lay in bed, Callie thought about what it must mean to be not just good-looking but as stunning as everyone seemed to agree Fiona had been, as well as clever. The medical student she knew had been mentally fragile as well as beautiful; did that apply to Fiona as well? Or had she been more like others Callie had also known, with a sense of entitlement because they knew they were beautiful? Entitlement to the best-looking and richest boyfriends just because you could take them and therefore also an entitlement to all the good things in life: nice cars, the best restaurants and designer clothes. Had Fiona possibly thought that she deserved a partnership even if she hadn't worked for it? Was she so used to getting her own way all the time that when the tide turned against her and Giles wouldn't give her a partnership, like the medical student who got behind with her studies, she couldn't cope?

As she lay there, Callie wondered if perhaps, again like the medical student, Fiona had had a breakdown of some sort after the debacle at Townsend Bartlett. That was certainly something she could try and check: see if she had been treated in any local psychiatric units. Like the woman whose name was used by the downstairs tenant. Now that would certainly be a good place to start looking, as there simply had to be a reason why her identity was chosen. It was all starting to make sense.

Happy to have a course of action planned for herself, Callie finally fell asleep.

Chapter 26

It was not until after a particularly long and difficult surgery the next morning that Callie found the time to try and contact Mervyn Bartlett. Unsurprisingly, he didn't answer on any of the phone numbers she had for him and she ended up just leaving a message with the new receptionist at Townsend Bartlett, who told her that Mervyn was working from home that day.

Callie wondered how long it would take before the name was changed to Bartlett Hersham, or even Hersham Bartlett, because she had no doubt that Antonia would want that eventually. Or would she give up on the practice, even though she was now a partner, in light of Mervyn's troubles? Callie couldn't see her still wanting to be associated with them now that both Townsend and Bartlett had been publicly outed, even if in Mervyn's case it wasn't true, possibly wasn't true. The press certainly was not holding back with its opinion of the firm, which had been dubbed 'The Pervert Partners'.

She tried to explain to the receptionist that she wanted to speak to Mervyn with a view to proving his innocence, but she was pretty sure that that part of the message would not be passed on, so she had little hope that he would return her call.

It looked as though door-stepping him, as she had done with Doreen Ponting, was going to be the only way she would get to speak to Mervyn Bartlett. His address was not in the phone book, probably so that disgruntled clients couldn't bring their complaints to his door.

It was a good thing that Callie was armed with the electoral roll disk that she had picked up from Kate on her way into work, and despite the computer's best efforts to stop her reading what was on it, she managed to bypass the security and look. Result! Although the information on the disk was about five years out of date, not only did she find Mervyn Bartlett's home address, she also found a local address for Fiona Hutchins.

It was frustrating that she had no time to visit either just yet. She had a full surgery and, for the first time in months, two invitations to go out.

The first was for her regular Friday night out with Kate, who was currently between men.

And the second was with Billy. A proper date for dinner at Webbe's. She had been sufficiently surprised by the request to say yes before she remembered her vow never to go out with someone she worked with again. Too late to back down. She just hoped she was right and that he wasn't the type to cause problems when it all went horribly wrong. As it always did, in Callie's experience.

"Hi, Kate?" she said into the phone as she riffled through her wardrobe trying to decide what to wear. It was a long-held rule for both of them that dates came first on a Friday, but only if they met up the next morning for brunch and a post-mortem of the event in their favourite café.

"So, eleven o'clock in The Land of Green Ginger? You're paying." Kate had agreed and left Callie to her indecision about clothes.

* * *

They met in The Crown, which was crowded, and it was difficult to find a seat. Fortunately, the weather had improved and they took their drinks outside.

"Are you sure you're warm enough?" Billy asked.

"Yes, fine, thank you. It's nice to get away from the noise."

Unfortunately, some of the crowds and noise had followed them outside and there was the added irritation of cigarette smoke.

They moved a little further along the pavement.

"At least it's stopped raining," she ventured, and he nodded. They both sipped their wine. It was strange how she and Billy had found conversation so easy when they were just out as friends but that now they were on an actual date, it was much harder; even stilted. She looked down at her outfit. Her decision to go casual, in jeans with a silk blouse, seemed too dressed down compared to the smart chinos and jacket that Billy was wearing.

Callie took another sip of wine. A little alcohol would undoubtedly make the conversation flow more easily, but she didn't want to get drunk. Not on a first date, anyway. *Why was dating so hard?* she asked herself.

"It's hard, isn't it?" Billy said with a smile, mirroring her thoughts. "This whole first date thing."

"Very," she agreed with a smile. "Knowing what to wear."

"You look perfect," he said gallantly. "I am overdressed by contrast. I was nervous."

"About what?" Callie knew it wasn't only women who had dating anxieties, but this openness about it, from a man, was a first.

"What to wear, where to go," he admitted. "Is Webbe's okay, by the way?"

"Perfect," she reassured him, then wiggled her glass. "And then there's knowing how much to drink or not to drink."

He laughed.

"The things we worry about." He shook his head and checked his watch.

"Want to call it a day already?" she asked, only half-joking, anxiously playing with her glass.

"I was thinking we could stand here for an hour and then go to Webbe's and make excruciating conversation for an hour, each trying not to say anything out of turn, wondering if we want to go further or not, or if the other might not want to, or alternatively, we could grab a takeaway and bottle of wine and go back to yours, or mine, whichever, and just see where the evening leads us."

He looked anxious as Callie didn't reply for a moment while she thought about his suggestion. All in all, it seemed a very sensible one.

"Mine. It's closer, just up the hill," she finally said. "I have wine and we can call for a takeaway."

He grinned and grabbed her hand. They left their drinks and hurried up the steps to the top of the East Hill.

* * *

In the event, they never did get around to ordering a takeaway.

Billy left early the next morning for football training with the five-a-side team he played for, promising to see her for Sunday lunch and a walk if the weather was fine. That meant that Callie had had a leisurely morning, with tea in bed and a smile on her face.

She was still smiling as she entered The Land of Green Ginger Café and saw Kate sitting at a corner table.

"No need to ask how the date went then," Kate said and went back to perusing the menu. The waitress gave them some time to decide before coming over.

"Very well, thank you," Callie replied regardless and also picked up the menu.

"Sausage breakfast and a large latte, please," Kate ordered when the waitress came over for their order.

"Poached eggs and tomatoes on wholemeal toast," Callie added. "And tea. Thank you." The waitress sighed. It was exactly what they always wanted.

Once Callie had finished telling Kate how wonderful Billy was and Kate had stopped pretending to gag, a move that had worried the waitress so much that she had come over to ask if their breakfast was all right; having reassured her that Kate wasn't gagging because of the food, they moved onto the subject of the lawyer incidents and what Callie was doing about it.

"Have you told Steve Miller everything, yet?" Kate asked as she wiped her plate clean with a piece of toast.

"I still think it's too early. I want to give Ms Ponting the chance to find out a bit more about Fiona, although," she said with a glint in her eye, "I do have an address for her."

"It was on the disk?" Kate asked in amazement.

"Yup," Callie answered smugly. "I went to find Mervyn Bartlett's home address, so I checked for hers as well and there it was, Markwick Terrace, in St Leonards." Just as it had when she had first seen the address, she felt a little ping of recognition, but she couldn't for the life of her remember where she had heard the name before.

Kate wiped her mouth decorously with a napkin and reached for her coat.

"Right by the park? What are we waiting for? Let's go and check it out."

Chapter 27

The house on Markwick Terrace wasn't hard to find. Far from being one of the imposing, white-painted terrace of Edwardian villas that were built when the road was new, Fiona's address was a rather later addition – a detached house in need of some repair and a good gardener, if only to cut back some of the bushes. There was a builder's van parked outside. As well as a sign from a local estate agent telling them the house had been sold. Callie's heart sank.

Not so easily put off, Kate walked up to the open front door and called out, "Hello?"

A middle-aged man wearing a grubby T-shirt that was stretched over an enormous beer belly and failed to reach his sagging, paint-stained jeans, came out to speak to them.

"Yes, love?" He enquired as he hauled his jeans up, attempting and failing to get them to meet the bottom of his shirt.

"I saw the *Sold* sign outside and wondered if you could tell me who had bought it?"

The builder scratched his head.

"Not sure about that, love."

"Only, you see, I was out of the country, otherwise I would have bought it myself as I've always wanted to live here, since I was a child. I thought I might offer to buy it off them." She looked around. "As they obviously haven't moved in yet."

The man smiled.

"Could be you're in luck then, only it was a builder what bought it. My boss. He's doing it up to sell. Terrible state it was in. Old lady had lived here for years, never done a thing to it since her hubbie died in year dot." The builder paused to scratch himself in a delicate area.

"I knew the daughter once and I would have thought she would have wanted to live here, but perhaps it had too many memories." Kate was really getting into her role.

"Don't know nuffink about a daughter. The boss might. He bought it after the old lady died. There was delays though, something legal had to happen."

"Probate?" Kate asked, ever the solicitor.

"Yeh, somefink like that." He seemed to have grown bored of the conversation and rummaged about in his front pocket and finally pulled out a creased and dirty business card. "You'll need to speak to the boss. Let him know you want to buy the place. It might save him estate agent fees, which will please him. His number's here, I gotta get back to work." He handed over the card and disappeared back inside.

* * *

"That was a bit of a dead loss," Callie said as they walked away from the house.

"Not at all," Kate said brightly.

"But she doesn't live here anymore."

"No, but where there's probate there's probably a will, or at any rate, an awful lot of paperwork that is part of the public record. I'll be able to look it all up for you. Who owned the house, who she left all her worldly goods to, who the solicitor was who settled everything, including sorting out the money going to the legatees. If he handed out the money, he must know where to find them."

"You're thinking that Fiona lived here with her mother."

"It's got to be a possibility, hasn't it? She gave it as her address on the electoral roll. Leave it with me, I'll see what I can dig up."

"Knowing my luck, old Mrs Hutchins left it all to a cats home."

"I had a client once, left it all to Battersea Dogs Home. Now that, I can understand."

The conversation had rung another bell with Callie and this time she remembered why.

"Lady Markwick!" she exclaimed.

Kate gave her an odd look.

"Who?" Kate asked. "And what about her?"

"I knew the name rang a bell. It was the name of Mrs Townsend's dog – well, one of them, anyway."

"So, she names her dogs after local landmarks, or historical figures. It's not unusual."

"But it's a bit of a coincidence she chose a name closely connected to our main suspect, don't you think?"

"You think she'd name her dog after the place where her husband's lover lived?"

"It does seem unlikely," Callie agreed. "Even if she didn't like him very much."

But as they drove back towards Hastings and Callie dropped Kate off at her cottage, Callie couldn't shake the coincidence from her mind.

* * *

Mrs Townsend's house was just as imposingly neo-gothic as she remembered it. The morning's sunshine had given way to cloud and it was a damp, grey afternoon, which suited the location perfectly. It almost made it seem threatening. Half-expecting Count Dracula to suddenly appear from the bushes, Callie was relieved to see a car parked outside the front door, so at least it seemed likely that someone was at home.

The cacophony of dog barks that greeted her door knock was no different from the last time she had been here. This time it managed to dispel the aura of gloom, now that she knew it wasn't the hound of the Baskervilles waiting on the other side of the door.

"Oh. I wasn't expecting you." Mrs Townsend answered the door with her usual degree of bluntness.

"No, I was just passing and popped in because I wanted to ask you something, I hope you don't mind," Callie said, restraining herself from asking exactly whom Mrs Townsend might have been expecting. In turn, Mrs Townsend didn't ask her how on earth she was 'just passing' when the house was not on the way to anywhere.

She showed Callie into the same room she and Mike Parton had sat in when they visited before. It seemed much the same, apart from a different half-chewed dog toy left on the armchair.

"You are all right with dogs, aren't you?" Mrs Townsend asked but didn't wait for Callie to reply before going back to release the dogs from their imposed exile in the back of the house.

As Tucker and Lady M came bounding in, Callie prepared herself. She was glad she was wearing jeans and not easily shreddable tights this time around, particularly as it was a second meeting and both dogs assumed that meant she was a friend of the family; probably a long-lost friend of the family. Tucker jumped up on the chair beside her and Lady M, once she had stopped bouncing up and down on the spot and turning in circles of joy, settled down and rested a paw on Callie's knee.

"Hello again, Lady Markwick," Callie said, shaking the proffered paw with one hand and holding off the over-enthusiastic welcome from Tucker with the other.

Harriet Townsend sat in the chair opposite. If she was surprised at Callie remembering her dog's name, she didn't show it.

"Down, you two. Leave Dr Hughes alone," she said half-heartedly.

"It's fine," Callie answered, lying. It wasn't Lady M she was concerned about but Tucker, who was being an absolute nuisance in an effort to lick her face. "I like dogs." She smiled to back up this statement and thought that Mrs Townsend looked at her with a slightly friendlier air. It seemed to have a magic effect on Tucker, too. It was as if he realised that he wasn't going to get a reaction from Callie so he might as well give up, and he jumped down and went to sit at Mrs Townsend's feet. Lady M just rested her nose on Callie's knee and looked at her with an expression that said: please, please love me. Callie found herself gently stroking the dog in response.

"So, why are you here, Dr Hughes? I take it you didn't just come to see my dogs."

"Well, in a way, I have come to see you about the dogs," Callie answered. She had thought long and hard in an effort to come up with a plan to ask about Lady Markwick's provenance without seeming to, but in the end had decided that all her ideas were ridiculous, and that honesty was probably the best policy. "I came to ask you about Lady M here, and how she got her name?"

If Mrs Townsend was surprised by the question, she hid it well.

"I've no idea. I didn't name her," she replied bluntly. "I do know that the Markwick family were related to the Eversfields, who were local developers in the nineteenth century, I believe, so I suspect it was after them."

"Perhaps the person who named her was actually associated with the Markwick family?" Callie fished but Mrs Townsend looked blank. "Or perhaps lived near the park?" she suggested as she looked into the dog's liquid eyes and gently rubbed the bridge of her nose. Lady M closed her eyes in ecstasy.

When she looked up, Callie saw that Mrs Townsend was looking at her in a hard and appraising way, as if deciding what to do, and say, next. A small shiver ran through Callie as she realised that perhaps it had not been a good idea to come out to such an isolated house on her own, especially as she had not told anyone where she was going. Mrs Townsend could have been involved in the murder of her own husband. After all, she had been damaged by his actions as well as Fiona. But if she was involved, Callie thought, she would have done something not quite so damaging to her own reputation.

"You are quite right, of course." The reply came eventually. It seemed that Mrs Townsend had decided that a little honesty was in order as well. "I inherited Lady M when her owner, whose family lived near Markwick Gardens, had to be admitted to a psychiatric hospital. Sad story. Her mother couldn't cope with the dog, so I said I'd take her in."

"And she was happy with that? Fiona, I mean?" Callie said, letting Mrs Townsend know that she knew who the dog's previous owner had been. Callie had put the story together on her way over; it was just too much of a coincidence otherwise. At least she hoped it was.

"Oh, good heavens, no. She would never have allowed me to have her. Not after–" Mrs Townsend stopped short of actually saying after what. "I believe her mother told her the dog had gone to a rescue centre and been rehomed. As far as I am aware, she never knew where."

"You knew her mother?"

"I got to know her when Fiona was clearly unwell. Someone had to do something. The girl was a danger to herself, going around saying such silly things. Mrs Hutchins understood."

Callie wondered just how much money had been wafted under Mrs Hutchins' nose to help her understand. However, it seemed a pretty good explanation of how the dog had come to be in Mrs Townsend's possession.

"I can understand why Fiona would never allow you to have Lady M. After all, why would she let her rapist's wife take her dog?"

There was a tense silence which Lady M seemed to sense, her eyes asking if everything was all right; was it still okay to take affection from this visitor?

"I think you will find rape implies a lack of consent."

"She may have consented to having sex with your husband but only to save her career. Sex under duress is still rape in my world."

"You only have her word for the duress. My husband had a different story. She threw herself at him and when he turned her down, she started inventing these stories." Her voice was so laden with contempt that Lady M gave a little squeak of distress. "I take it you've spoken to her?"

"No!" Callie was surprised into saying. "I've been trying to find her. I thought you might be able to help."

"And why on earth would I want to help you find that… that bitch?"

"Because I think Giles's murder had something to do with her."

That shocked Mrs Townsend into silence.

"What on earth makes you think that?" she asked eventually.

"As you say, she accused him of rape. I mean, look at the personal nature of the way he was killed, and the way she has also done her best to make things embarrassing for you, and the firm."

"Do you think she's behind Mervyn's latest disaster too?"

"Yes, and some others. The head of the CPS; a corporate lawyer from London."

"There was an incident at the firm she worked at in London, I remember," Mrs Townsend told Callie. "When she joined Townsend Bartlett she'd had some time off. She explained it away as some sort of a belated gap year, but when I asked where she'd been, what she'd done in that year, she was always evasive. That's what made me think she'd had a breakdown before."

"I don't suppose you remember the name of the firm she worked for in London, do you?"

"Let me see." Mrs Townsend thought for a while. "It was a person's name, a family name, I seem to remember, which is unusual for a corporation in this day and age; everyone nowadays seems to be a three letter acronym, even though no one probably remembers what the letters originally stood for. That or something totally bland and inoffensive in any possible language, and that has absolutely no meaning in any of them. It's only small firms like Townsend Bartlett that still use family names."

Callie agreed wholeheartedly, although she thought that shortening the firm to TB probably wouldn't bring in the sort of custom they were hoping for. She said nothing because she didn't want to disturb the older woman's train of thought.

"Walker, Williams? No, it was a longer name than that."

Callie desperately wanted to help her by suggesting the name she was hoping it was, but bit her tongue.

"Warlingham? No. Westerham, no. Got it!" She clicked her fingers and shouted out so suddenly that both dogs jumped up and barked. "Wendlesham's. I'm sure it was Wendlesham's."

Callie could have cheered.

"Who, coincidentally, have recently had a senior lawyer murdered and another collapsed in a gay sauna – oh, and some very damaging emails were sent to their clients. Do you believe me now when I say that I think Fiona is behind all this?"

It was clear from her expression that Mrs Townsend did indeed believe her.

"My God! When I think of all I've gone through because of her!"

Callie didn't like to remind the woman that Fiona had gone through quite a bit courtesy of her husband as well.

Chapter 28

Having made plans to spend her Sunday with Billy, Callie was disappointed to wake up to see that the rain had set in, making a walk across the cliffs a non-starter. Instead, they spent the day in her flat, talking, making love, talking, eating takeaway Thai and talking some more.

They had talked about the case, about sexual harassment, careers and casual racism. And much, much more. He had told her his full name was Bilal Iqbal and she had admitted to Calliope and even to a middle name of Harriet, although they both probably already knew each other's full names from checking the medical register, LinkedIn and other lists. In Callie's case, not just checking out Billy's medical background, but checking for any mention of a wife, having been caught out that way before, although she wasn't about to admit that to Billy.

When Billy had finally left, at five o'clock, Callie had spent most of a fruitless half hour trying to get hold of Miller, leaving messages around the police station and on his work phone that she was sure would never reach him.

"That man can be very elusive when he wants to be," she grumbled to Kate on the phone later that evening. "Have you managed to find out about the will?"

"Give a girl a chance." Kate laughed. "I spent the afternoon at the gym."

"Oh yes?" Callie asked suspiciously, knowing that Kate rarely went to the gym to exercise.

"I'm meeting him later," her friend confided. "You see? You aren't the only one with a date."

The call was necessarily a short one, as Kate had to get ready to meet her latest conquest. Suddenly at a loose end, Callie wondered what to do with the rest of her evening. She could microwave a dinner and watch television, she could have a long bath and an early night, catch up on some housework, or she could carry on with her detecting as she waited for Miller to respond to her messages. Whatever, she needed to do something to stop herself from compulsively checking her phone for messages from Billy, or worse, messaging him every five minutes when she knew he was at a family dinner.

* * *

The driveway outside Mervyn Bartlett's modern detached house on the outskirts of Hastings was empty. The house looked every bit as closed and empty as Doreen Ponting's had done. The curtains were drawn tightly shut at every window and not a single chink of light could be seen from any of them. Hoping that simply meant that he was hiding in the back of the house rather than that he had left the area, Callie parked in the driveway and approached the door.

Mervyn was a tougher nut to crack than Ms Ponting, it seemed. It took Callie several knocks on the door as well as holding her finger on the bell for a full minute as a final resort before he came to the door and shouted through it that she should stop harassing them and that he was calling the police.

"Mr Bartlett. It's Callie. Callie Hughes? I am with the police? Do you remember? I was at Giles Townsend's flat when you were there and again at the inquest opening."

There was silence for a few moments.

"What do you want?" he asked through the door.

"To talk to you about Fiona Hutchins and why she's set you up," Callie told him and was rewarded after a short while by the door opening a few inches. Mervyn's face stared out from the small gap and he checked she was who she said she was and that he couldn't see anyone else anywhere around.

"I'm here alone," she reassured him and was rewarded by the door closing as he unlatched the chain and then opened it wide to let her in.

As soon as she was inside the hallway, he closed the door, locking and bolting it and hurrying back to the rear of the house. Callie didn't know his personal circumstances, but the furnishings and dried flower display on the hall table suggested at least a Mrs Bartlett, while the assortment of trainers on and around the shoe rack and the games console attached to the TV in the living room suggested there might be children too. However, the strange stillness of the house told her that if so, they had all moved out for the time being.

They sat in the spacious living room, which had a pleasant, lived-in feel to it. Mervyn sat, stiff and awkward, in an armchair, constantly wringing his hands. The haunted expression that had been on his face when he first opened the door had now been replaced by one of quiet desperation.

"What makes you think this is all down to Fiona?" he asked.

Callie went through the same story she had told Mrs Townsend, adding in the details that she had learnt from her.

Mervyn let his head sink in his hands and groaned quietly.

"I told Giles not to do it!" he finally said.

"Not to do what?" Callie asked.

"Not to try it on with her, not after what happened in London, but he didn't listen, he never listened to me."

"What did happen in London?" she asked gently.

"From what I was told by John Dixon, it was just a bit of horseplay that got out of hand. A drunken celebration when they closed a big deal; you know what those city types are like. Work ridiculous hours under great stress, and when they let their hair down, well, they party hard and Fiona was, well, as I say, things went too far." He couldn't look her in the eye as he said this.

"She was raped?"

"Let's just say, she didn't say no, but she might not have been in a fit state to give her consent."

"She was raped then," Callie said clearly and firmly. She hated the mealy-mouthed way that he was avoiding saying that word: 'horseplay that went too far', 'she didn't actually say no'. Rape was still rape, no matter how you phrased it.

Mervyn just shrugged and said, "Technically, yes." He looked at her for a moment before his eyes slid away again. "What made it worse, I imagine, was that she only knew about it when pictures circulated in the office the next day."

Callie sighed. This was just awful, she thought, far worse than she had imagined and it made her angrier than ever. The poor woman.

"And I suppose the man who 'technically' raped her was Adrian Cole?"

Mervyn looked up, startled.

"How did you know?"

"Oh, the fact that he was found dead in Mr Wendlesham's swimming pool a few days ago might have been a clue," she said harshly. "What did John Dixon have to do with it?"

Mervyn was too shocked to hear of Cole's death, which hadn't made the news in any big way, to answer for a moment.

"Adrian? Dead? How did that happen?"

"It's a long story with lots of suspicious circumstances. But you see why I think Fiona is involved now?"

He gave a deep sigh and nodded.

"John said she wanted to lodge a formal complaint, and go to the police, which would have been very bad for the firm. So, he dissuaded her, for her own good, and organised the NDA and payoff," Mervyn admitted. "Oh God! She must have set him up in the massage place as well. She did, didn't she?"

"I rather think he went there himself, although she may have drugged him and organised for the press to be there when he was carried out. That seems to be the pattern," she told Mervyn. "The rapists have both been killed and the people who helped them to keep it quiet and get away with it have all been humiliated in some way." Callie refrained from adding, 'like Fiona was humiliated by the pictures of her drunken state and sexual assault circulated with the morning coffee'.

Mervyn dropped his head in his hands again.

"Humiliated? That doesn't even begin to cover it. We should never have taken her on." His self-pity was nauseating.

"I did wonder why on earth you did."

"It was a favour to John. Apparently, she'd had a bit of a breakdown after the event." He was still unwilling to call it rape. "She took some time off which she could afford to do as the payoff was very handsome."

Callie clenched her teeth to stop herself from asking him exactly how handsome a pay-out had to be to make rape and public humiliation acceptable.

"The gap in her employment meant most places wouldn't touch her."

"And Giles's past history of sexual harassment didn't raise any red flags for you?"

Mervyn did at least look a little guilty at that.

"He always denied it. I mean, he admitted he touched the girl, but not in a sexual way," he said.

Callie again stopped herself from saying, 'well he would do, wouldn't he?'

"I did tell him to leave her alone," he added.

"You thought telling a sexual predator to stop would be enough?"

"I didn't think of him as a predator; I just didn't want him upsetting Fiona and setting her off again."

"Flashing the receptionists is fine to your mind, but I am pleased to hear that you do draw the line at him coercing more senior staff into having sex with him."

"He didn't mean any harm with the junior staff. He was always a bit of a character."

"A bit of a character? I can certainly see why Fiona might think you facilitated Giles's sexual harassment of staff." Callie could hardly control her anger. It was people like Mervyn who allowed sexual predators and bullies to get away with it for so long.

"I did not facilitate it."

"But you did absolutely nothing to stop it, did you?"

Mervyn couldn't reply to that. He looked beaten. He must have realised that his actions, or rather inaction, was what had led to his current situation.

"Do you know which psychiatric unit she was admitted to?" Callie asked him.

"Gable Leighs," he told her. "It's a private clinic. We paid," he added, as if paying for the treatment made up for driving your employees into a breakdown. "But she left there about four months ago."

"And you don't know where she is now?"

"No." He shrugged.

"She used to live with her mother in Markwick Terrace, she might be there," he suggested, not knowing that Callie had already been to that address.

* * *

It was a tired and thoughtful Callie who finally arrived home at eleven o'clock and flopped on her sofa. She rubbed her forehead in an effort to dispel the headache that was fast taking hold. She knew there was no point trying to sleep with all these thoughts whirring through her head. She needed to think things through before she would be able to drop off.

She had sympathy for, and empathy with, Fiona Hutchins. They had a lot in common. Good-looking, clever and career-minded, but Callie acknowledged that when it came to looks, she probably wasn't in the same class as Fiona – after all, everyone had said the lawyer was stunningly beautiful – but there were enough similarities for Callie to understand that it could make life more difficult. Fiona probably craved affection and perhaps that came across as being available, or wanting sex even. Not that that was in any way an excuse for her treatment by the two men, or for the lack of support she was shown by their colleagues. To be treated so badly, and then to have the final blow, being forced to sign a non-disclosure agreement meaning that you could never tell anyone what had happened, never say why you had had a breakdown, why you were unable to work for so long, why you could never trust a man again. That must have been doubly, impossibly hard. Theoretically Fiona should not have even told her therapist what had happened if she had signed an NDA, but Callie hoped to goodness she had done.

In the past, Callie had had difficult moments with regards to sexual harassment herself. There had been a tutor who wanted to sleep with her, and suggested it might help her grades, but when she refused, he didn't mark her down, or up, in case she reported him; at least she hoped not. He accepted that he'd tried it on and failed. And she'd had to change driving instructors when the first one kept putting his hand on her knee, and not in an avuncular way. She'd never reported these incidents, or these men, and thought now that she should have done. At the time, she had argued that to ruin their careers over something that small would be harsh, but what about the students who came after her?

Unlike Fiona, she had never been raped while drunk and incapable, or forced to have sex just to keep her job, but she realised that perhaps being beautiful was as much of a curse as a benefit.

At last, Callie began to feel tired. She had been over the terrible story of Fiona's rapes enough and she was left with an overwhelming sense of pity for a woman whose life had been ruined.

Finally, she felt she could try going to bed, and got up from the sofa. It was then that she noticed that the light on her answerphone was flashing, which meant another dilemma: she would never be able to sleep knowing there were unheard messages, but equally, listening to the message might have the same effect of ending all hope of sleep. And standing there debating whether or not to listen to the message wasn't helping either.

Irritated, she jabbed at the play button.

"Hi, it's me." Miller's voice came out of the machine. The sound quality was poor. He was obviously using handsfree while driving. "Sorry about not getting back to you earlier, but things are really busy. Look, there's something I should tell you—" There was a noise in the background, and it sounded like Miller had come to a halt and was switching off the engine. "I'll try to get back to you again when I have some time. Bye."

Callie sat back down on the sofa, pressed the play button to listen to the message again and tried to analyse the words, and the tone in which they were said.

What did he mean by busy? With the case? Or with his wife? Was he sad? Did he sound tired? No, she decided, he'd sounded irritated. Presumably at having to deal with her calls and messages when he had better things to do. He clearly didn't understand that she was trying to help, that she could help. And now he'd made her angry and if there was one thing that was guaranteed to stop her from sleeping, it was being angry!

Chapter 29

It was Monday morning before Callie tried to get hold of Miller again. She was already in danger of running late for work but she tried to reach him on his mobile before leaving her flat.

"Hello, you're through to Detective Inspector Miller, please leave a message after–" She hung up, dropped the phone into her bag and picked her car keys up from the table. Detective Inspector Miller would have to wait. She was in too good a mood after her lovely day with Billy on Sunday. It wasn't until she took a late lunchbreak that Callie had time to try calling him, and got an answerphone message again.

"This is ridiculous," she told herself before grabbing her bag and heading off to the police station. If he wouldn't answer his ruddy phone, she had no choice but to try and beard him in his den.

* * *

Having waited a quarter of an hour at the front desk with her temper slowly rising, Callie was relieved when Jayne Hales finally came down from the incident room to collect her.

"Sorry about that, Dr Hughes; we're all at sixes and sevens today."

"Has something happened with the case?" Callie asked sharply.

"Not as such," Jayne said as she held a door open for Callie. "It's just that we seem to have mislaid the boss."

Callie was unable to comment, partly because she was struck dumb by the news and partly because they had arrived in the incident room.

She could see DS Jeffries in Miller's office, with an older man she recognised as Superintendent Orde. Jeffries was looking flustered and Orde... Well, Orde was looking downright furious.

As Callie hesitated, unsure whether or not to disturb them, Orde came out of Miller's office and walked briskly past her, a nod his only greeting as he hurriedly left the room.

Once he was out of sight, Jeffries came out of Miller's office and looked theatrically around.

"All clear, is it?" he asked and was met by a nervous laugh from the rest of the CID staff in the room.

Jeffries looked at Callie.

"Don't suppose you know where the boss is?" he asked. "Not hiding under your bed, is he?"

"No," she said, choosing to ignore his insinuation. "In fact, I came here to give him a piece of my mind for ignoring me. Oh, that, and to tell him I know who killed Giles Townsend and Adrian Cole." She had so wanted to say that in front of Miller, to see his face when she said she was right all along and she had solved his case for him. Unfortunately, the moment wasn't nearly as good with Jeffries as stand in. There was a murmur of interest from those in the room, but if Jeffries was surprised, he covered it well.

"So, come on, Doc. Tell us all who did it." He sat on the edge of a desk, causing a pile of papers to fall off, but not even bothering to pick them up or apologise to DC

Nigel Nugent whose desk it apparently was and who spent the next few minutes picking up and sorting all the paper that had fallen. Callie explained about Fiona Hutchins and what had happened at Wendlesham's and then at Townsend Bartlett.

For the first time ever, DS Jeffries didn't even interrupt her with a crass or sexist comment.

"So, you reckon this Fiona is the one who killed the two of them and set the others up?"

"I know it seems hard to—"

"She's supposed to be drop-dead gorgeous and all the victims knew her, but no witness saw anyone like her and none of the victims say anyone involved is her. Don't you think that's a bit strange?"

"But—" It was the weak point of her story, Callie knew. However, Jeffries wasn't about to let her finish telling them why she thought it had to be Fiona.

"Don't get me wrong," he said. "I admit it must have something to do with her. It's just that I think we'd have noticed someone that much of a looker if she was hanging round, especially the boss."

"But you will investigate her? Find out where she is now?"

"Too bloody right. Just as soon as we find out where the hell he is, I'm sure we'll be right on it."

He stood up, dismissing her, and Callie turned to walk towards the door, before stopping.

"Why did you say that?"

"Say what?" Jeffries seemed surprised.

"About 'especially the boss'. Why would he have noticed her especially?"

"Because he was the senior investigating officer," he explained. "When she tried to bring charges against Townsend. Believe me, Doc, we all wanted to see Townsend go down for shagging her, but the CPS wouldn't go for it."

Callie walked slowly back towards Jeffries as she processed what he had just said.

"You're telling me that he was part of the team that failed to prosecute Giles Townsend for rape, along with Townsend who is dead and Doreen Ponting who was set up? And he just happens to have gone missing? You don't think that perhaps she might have just gone after him as well?"

There was an uncomfortable silence, as everyone looked at Jeffries.

"That's not fucking likely, is it?" But he sounded flustered. "I mean, the boss? He's probably just got a problem with his old lady."

"Then why hasn't he let us know?" Jayne interjected. "And why doesn't his wife know anything about it?" Jeffries raised his eyebrows. "I just spoke to her. She's staying at her sister's for a few days, has no idea where the DI is."

"I can't believe this." Jeffries shook his head. "Why him? He did his best to get the CPS to charge Townsend."

"But he failed. And to Fiona he's just another person who has let all this happen to her."

"You think she's going to kill him?" Jayne asked.

Callie shook her head.

"That's not her pattern. Only the actual perpetrators have been killed. Everyone else has just been embarrassed in some way."

"Right." Jeffries was suddenly decisive. "Let's get everybody on this and find the boss before the press get pictures of him with his trousers down. Nigel, see if his car pinged any ANPR cameras. The rest of you, get checking CCTV, see if you can spot him."

"What time period?" someone asked.

"From when he left here, gone ten last night, and when he should have been here at eight this morning," Jayne answered and Jeffries nodded.

"Could we try and get the phone company to track his phone?" Jeffries asked Nigel, who was the resident guru for anything technical like that.

"They're going to demand a warrant, which will take a while, but I can get started on that," Nigel agreed. "Also, I can ask IT to get into the DI's computer and check his emails, see if there's anything there."

Jeffries looked horrified.

"Can they do that?"

"His work ones? Of course." Nigel seemed surprised to be even asked the question and Callie could see Jeffries mentally checking what they might find if they looked at his emails before dismissing the thought.

"Jayne, let's start at his home, see if we can find any clues there."

As they all hurried to their allotted tasks, Callie was left standing there like a spare part. Desperately worried as she was, she knew that she had nothing more to contribute, so she turned and left them to their search.

* * *

Outside, once Callie was sitting in her car, she took out her phone. She always kept it on silent when in the surgery and had forgotten to turn the ringer back on, but she had felt it buzz while she was talking to Jeffries. There was a missed call and voice message from Kate. She waved at Jayne as she and Jeffries drove out of the car park on their way to Miller's house and listened as the phone connected with her voice mail.

"Hi Callie," came Kate's cheery voice. "I've taken a look at the will and probate documents and Fiona's address is given as Castle Cottage, Lye Lane, Bodiam, so you will be able to deliver the whole case to the sultry Steve all tied up with a bow. If that doesn't make him eternally grateful, nothing will. Ciao!"

Bodiam was a small village about ten miles from Hastings, famous for its fourteenth-century castle, built to defend the area from an invasion by France.

Callie hesitated. There was no way she could get there and back before evening surgery. She could let Nigel and the incident room team know the address and leave them to follow it up, but they were all busy with their own search and it might be a while before they could get someone there. In the end, she compromised by sending a text message to Jayne giving her the address and saying she was going to check it out, and then rang the surgery.

"Hi Linda," she said. "You're not going to like this but—"

As predicted, Linda did not like Callie pulling out of her evening surgery at such short notice.

"I'm sorry but it's a police emergency," Callie explained. "You know I can never predict when I'll be needed." Callie had her fingers crossed as she allowed Linda to believe that this was really an emergency with her police job, even though she knew there was no way that this expedition would be classified as part of her role.

But she couldn't help worrying. What if Fiona really did have Miller in her clutches? What if she was setting him up like she had done to both Doreen and Mervyn? The press could have already been alerted, incriminating photos could imminently be appearing online. Time was definitely of the essence if she was going to stop it happening again. Having left Linda the task of cancelling as many patients as possible and re-allocating others to Callie's colleagues who, no doubt, would want some return favours like covering their weekends on call as a result, Callie started her car. There really was no time to lose if she was to stop Miller from being the latest victim.

Chapter 30

As she drove into Bodiam and turned right down Lye Lane towards the castle, Callie realised just how isolated this location was. Castle Cottage was only just visible from the road, situated as it was down a short track between fields. It certainly had no neighbours near enough to hear a scream or a shout for help. You'd have to hoist a flag saying 'Help!' and hope a passing car stopped to do so.

As Callie turned into the lane leading to the cottage, she saw that anyone in the house would know immediately that someone was coming, but it was too late to do anything about it. Parking in the main road and walking across the fields might have given her the element of surprise, but with all the rain in recent days she'd end up covered in mud and would probably still be seen from the cottage well before she reached it.

There were no other cars parked outside the quaint little house and Callie wondered if this was going to be a dead end in more ways than one, with no one at home, and that she might have cancelled her evening surgery for nothing. She checked her phone. No signal. Typical, she thought to herself as she parked the car and got out. A phone signal out in the country? That really would be asking too much. Another reason she could never live there.

The cottage seemed very quiet as Callie got out of the car and scrunched across the gravel to the front door. From there, she could see a car parked out of sight by the side of the garage. Her pulse quickened as she realized it was Miller's car.

There was no bell on the door frame, so Callie used the knocker and listened. She couldn't hear any response to her knocking, so she knocked again and called out, "Hello? Fiona? My name's Doctor Hughes. Please answer the door."

She listened again and this time she thought she heard a noise. Not the sound of footsteps as someone came to answer the door, but more of a strangled cry.

"Hello?" She called again and the sound became more urgent and louder. It was hard to understand but Callie thought she could just make out the word 'Help!'. That was enough for her and she tried the door. To her surprise, it opened.

Inside, the cottage was furnished with items more suited to the large house in Markwick Terrace than a small country cottage, making Callie feel sure that she had the right place. The sounds of distress continued and appeared to be coming from upstairs. Looking around for something to use as a weapon, just in case, Callie picked up a poker from the companion set beside the fireplace.

"Fiona?" she called out again. "If you're here, I'm coming upstairs. Is that okay?" She was rewarded by more strangled noises with no distinguishable words.

Upstairs there were only two doors leading off the small landing. Callie cautiously pushed the first door open to reveal a tiny bathroom. The second door was ajar, and she could see the end of a brass bed. As she pushed the door further open, she could see the whole of the large double bed, on which a man, stark naked, was spread-eagled. His wrists were tied to either side of the brass bedhead with velvet ribbon, and his feet were similarly attached to the smaller footboard. She moved towards the bed and noted that he had a small English rose tattoo just above his right breast, but no other identifying marks that she could see. Once Callie looked at the man's head, it became clear why he was unable to speak clearly. His head was encased in a gimp mask, complete with a ball in his mouth. The man wriggled and cried in distress, desperately trying to free himself.

"It's okay, I'll try and get you out of this," she said as she unzipped the mask and pulled it off.

"Jesus fucking Christ!" Miller said as he coughed and heaved with relief at being freed. Callie could only imagine how grim it must have been for him to lie there with the smell of rubber and the ball making it hard to breath and impossible to speak. As he continued to recover, Callie set about freeing him from the velvet ties on his wrists and feet. The knots were impossibly tight, probably worsened by his attempts to get out, and she had to run into the bathroom to find some nail scissors to cut them. Once he was freed, Miller rubbed his hands, trying to bring the feeling back, seemingly unaware or uncaring that he was completely naked. Callie tried not to look, but was pleased to note that he appeared to have all the right bits in all the right places.

There was the sound of cars crunching on gravel, and Callie looked out of the window.

"Looks like the press are here," she said. "And DS Jeffries." She turned back to see Miller clumsily pulling on the clothes that had been left on the floor. His hands were still numb from being tied up so long and he needed her help to do up his shirt buttons, although they left a number of them undone.

"Excuse me, sir," they heard Jeffries say outside the window. "This is a police matter and I would be grateful if you could wait outside."

"So would I," Miller said, and Callie was glad that he seemed to be feeling better.

Miller was still pulling on his trousers when they heard the sound of footsteps coming up the stairs.

"Hurry up," Callie said urgently, knowing that she would be the butt of jokes for years to come if she was caught in a bedroom with Miller in an undressed state.

The door opened.

"Hello, Sergeant Jeffries." Callie beamed, blocking his view as Miller finished doing up his fly behind her.

"Everything all right, boss?" Jeffries asked, peering round her. "Only, the gentlemen of the press downstairs seem to think you might have been involved in a bit of bondage."

His gaze went around the room, taking in the ties still on the bed and the gimp mask on the floor, the smirk on his face showing that he understood exactly how Callie had found his senior officer. Callie was sure she could see a tinge of regret in his eyes that he hadn't been the one to find and rescue him. He would have loved to have been able to hold that against Miller forever.

"I have no idea who it was that was involved in bondage here," Miller said with a degree of gravity that Callie found impressive under the circumstances. "But it certainly wasn't me."

* * *

"He was able to tell the press that they had received a tip-off that someone was being held at the cottage but that the person must have been able to free themselves and escape before the police arrived," Callie explained to Kate over a much needed drink later that night. "Of course, they couldn't really argue, because the man in the pictures they had been sent had on that gimp mask so they couldn't really know who it was."

"She is some piece of work, isn't she? I mean, you've got to hand it to her, she had him trussed up like a kipper.

Thank goodness you got there first. Although I'd never have given you the address if I'd thought for one moment that you were likely to go there on your own. Promise me you won't do that again, Callie. After all, she's a killer."

"I wouldn't have been in danger. She's only interested in the people she feels have done her wrong."

"But how on earth did she get Miller like that?"

"She called him, saying that she was the woman who lived downstairs from Giles Townsend. You know, the one who disappeared?"

Kate nodded.

"And that she had some information that might be relevant."

"And he wasn't suspicious?"

"Apparently not. She was offhand enough to convince him it was probably nothing, but he thought he'd better go out there and speak to her in case. Everyone else had knocked off for the night or were finishing up paperwork, so he went himself."

"And when he got there and discovered it wasn't the lady from downstairs?"

"Oh, but it was," Callie said triumphantly. "That's the amazing thing. He felt quite relaxed, knowing it wasn't Fiona, and accepted a cup of coffee. After that, he has only hazy recollections of what happened until he came to, tied to the bed and with a gimp mask on."

"So, the killer isn't Fiona? Is this woman someone she knows?"

"No, no. It was Fiona. Miller remembers enough of what she said before he passed out to realise that it had to be her. We've all been looking for this beautiful svelte blonde, but she's changed her appearance to the point of being unrecognisable."

Kate sat back in surprise.

"You're joking!"

"No. Honest. She's obviously put on a lot of weight, had a bad haircut and let her hair go back to its natural mousey brown. Really let herself go. If you imagine her not in the designer clothes everyone associated her with but in cheap, ill-fitting clothes as well, I'm not surprised no one recognised her."

"You'd think someone who knew her as well as Giles would have spotted something, the way she spoke or smiled or something."

"I think the trouble with being really truly beautiful, like Fiona was before her breakdown, is that no one actually remembers anything else about you," Callie said profoundly.

"Good job we don't have to worry about that, then," Kate replied with a grin.

"I'll drink to that," Callie said and they clinked glasses.

Chapter 31

In the days following Miller's close call, as Callie liked to refer to it, she was disappointed that he didn't contact her. She felt she was owed somewhat more than the brief moment he had taken to thank her at the cottage, once all the press had been sent away disappointed not to get another salacious story to grab the headlines. She wasn't sure the reporters had believed the story that an unknown man had been held prisoner but escaped before the police arrived, but they weren't going to risk being sued for saying the pictures they had been sent, along with the address of the cottage, featured Miller when they had no other evidence to support that allegation. It was certainly impossible to tell who was in the mask.

When Miller had thanked her that day, he'd seemed both relieved and embarrassed that it had been her who had found and freed him. Embarrassed to have been found naked, but relieved that it was her rather than the press, or Jeffries, and she could understand that. She could only imagine what Jeffries would have had to say about finding his boss, stark naked and tied up like a Christmas turkey. He would have regaled the canteen with the story for ever and a day. Callie was pretty sure Jeffries would have bribed one of the reporters to give him a copy of the picture anyway, because of course he knew it was Miller, even if the reporters weren't going to risk saying so, in which case, Miller might not have got that much of a reprieve.

Finally losing patience at being kept out of the loop, Callie called Jayne Hale to get an update on what was going on. Jayne happily told her that everyone in the different police forces involved in the various aspects of this investigation were looking for Fiona Hutchins now, but that none of them were having any success, even with the updated description. Jayne also told her that they finally all did believe the lawyer to be responsible for the deaths as well as the other events, and were busy collecting the evidence so that she could be charged once she was found.

The techies were sure that they would be able to link all email addresses used to contact her victims and send details to the press. And there were several common factors in the incidents apart from her history, as most of the victims could be connected to a mystery overweight woman immediately before their incident. She lived downstairs from Giles. She spoke to and then helped Doreen Ponting at the pub and could have spiked her drink. Witnesses had now come forward to say a woman with the same rough description was on the train with an absolutely paralytic Adrian Cole, apparently helping him, at exactly the time the emails had been sent from his phone, and also on an early morning train from the station near Compton's Cazeley after Cole's body was left in the pool. And she had been in the bar where John Dixon left his bottle of wine and glass unattended whilst he went to the lavatory. And of course, they knew she was at the cottage.

What amazed everyone was that none of her victims saw through her disguise, even though they all knew her. Callie had to admire the woman's ingenuity and found it hard to condemn her for her actions. What had been done to her had been so awful; Callie couldn't even begin to imagine how she would have reacted if it had been her rather than Fiona who was the victim. The frustration at not being able to see her assailants punished must have been simply overwhelming. Callie could never condone killing a fellow human being, no matter how awful a specimen they were, but that didn't mean she couldn't understand why someone might feel they had been left with no other choice.

If Callie was hurt that Miller didn't contact her to thank her for coming to his rescue, she tried not to show it, especially when she was with Billy, although, in truth, it wasn't hard to put it to the back of her mind when she was with Billy. It was Jayne who finally explained his lack of contact.

"The photos were sent to the boss's wife," she told Callie.

"But there was no way of her knowing who it was in the pictures," Callie said, and then remembered the English rose tattoo. Of course, the press wouldn't have been able to identify Miller but his own wife obviously would.

"Oh dear. I take it the pictures didn't go down well."

"I think that's probably an understatement," Jayne said tactfully. "You know, things are a bit" – she struggled to find the right word to describe the Millers' relationship – "volatile."

"Of course." Callie understood why he hadn't been in touch now. Calling another woman, let alone sending her flowers as a thank you, would only make matters worse if his wife was upset. She wondered if she really thought her husband had been complicit in the bondage session, or if she accepted that he had been drugged and placed in that position. Either way, Callie knew that it was going to take a lot of effort on Miller's part to smooth things over.

* * *

It was another lovely sunny afternoon, with just a hint of summer in the air, the kind of day that made you believe that winter really was on the way out. Callie and Billy were taking advantage of the fine weather and walking on the West Hill. Callie turned and took a deep breath, smiling as she took in the view of the Old Town. The sun was glinting off the sea and the gulls were wheeling overhead, and all was right with the world, it seemed to her.

"Almost as good as the view from your place," Billy said as he took her hand.

"Yes," she agreed. "But it's nice to get a different perspective every now and again."

They stopped for a while, Billy putting his sweatshirt on the damp grass for her to sit on.

"Are you going to be warm enough?" she asked, and he laughed.

"Of course! It's a lovely day."

And it was, she thought, as she closed her eyes and listened to the seagulls. Eventually, some clouds came over and they decided to go to the café at the top of the lift for tea and cake.

As they approached the café, Callie could see a small group of people gathering at the top of the lookout point above the teashop. Someone shouted, several others seemed to have their phones out, some to make calls, others to film whatever was going on. Callie looked at Billy and they both hurried on up there.

As they reached the top, Callie could see someone standing on the edge of the high rocks where she knew there was a dizzyingly steep drop.

"Shit," Billy said, as he pushed his way through the fast gathering crowd, closely followed by Callie. Once she was in front of the crowd, Callie could see that it was a woman standing very close to the edge, looking down.

"Don't!" she called out urgently and the woman turned around, wobbling slightly as she did so.

"Fiona!" Callie exclaimed. She recognised the woman standing on the edge as the person she had seen living downstairs from Giles Townsend. "Don't do it!"

Fiona gave a slight smile of recognition. The crowd hummed with expectation.

"At last!"

Callie was puzzled by the response. She moved forward, despite Billy touching her arm, wanting to hold her back but letting her go at the same time. She could feel his eyes boring into the back of her head, willing her to take care.

"Why do you say that? Were you expecting me to be here?"

Fiona shook her head.

"No. I meant, at last somebody actually recognises me as me." She sighed and looked around at the assembled people, but it was clear she wasn't seeing them. "When I was younger, slimmer, beautiful, people wanted to know me, they recognised me, they paid attention to me – too much attention."

"I know what happened to you, Fiona. I do understand."

"Do you? I doubt it. They didn't want to pay for what they did. No one wanted them to pay."

"I know, they should have listened, they should have–" Callie was edging closer as she spoke and could sense Billy moving forward too, trying to stay close to her, but not stopping her. Callie stopped as Fiona suddenly fixed her with a piercing look.

"Do you know what that CPS bitch said?" She was shaking with anger and stepped back to steady herself. Her foot was dangerously close to the edge and there was a collective gasp from the crowd behind Callie.

Callie shook her head and stayed still, holding her breath. Behind her, Billy stopped too.

"She said I should have known better." Fiona spat out the words. "Better than what? Better than to let my boss force me into bed? Or better than to have bothered reporting it?" She gave a short bark of empty laughter. "I should have known better."

Fiona looked down and round slightly, seeing how close she was to the ledge, testing the distance.

"When I came out of the psychiatric clinic, I thought that everyone would look at me and see someone who should have known better, but they didn't see that, they didn't see anything. In fact, I found they didn't see me at all." She looked at Callie. "You should try it. Put on a bit of weight." She laughed, looked at herself and then at Callie again. "Make that a lot of weight. Let yourself go. Leave the hair dye and makeup in the box. Stop bothering to pluck your eyebrows or shave your legs. You'll see. It's such a relief. Freedom. No one notices you. No one sees you. You become invisible. And the men? The men who pawed you and stroked you when you were beautiful? They don't even recognise you when you stand in front of them. All they ever saw was a beautiful woman, they never actually bothered to look at me as a person. It never occurred to any of them that this fat slag in front of them, saying good morning, serving them drinks, sitting next to them in a bar could be the beautiful Fiona Hutchins. It's been the perfect disguise."

"I know you. I recognised you," Callie told her.

"Ah, but you had never seen me before that day. The day you found Giles's body."

"I didn't find his body, it was the receptionist from the firm, wasn't it?" Callie edged forward again. "Why did you put her through that?"

"I did feel bad about it," Fiona admitted. "But I had to stop him before he did it to anyone else. Better to find a body, don't you think? Than to be assaulted?"

Callie didn't quite know what to say to that.

"I knew they would send someone over when he was late for work and not answering his phone. I knew she would be young. They all were. And I was sure it wouldn't be a receptionist that knew me, as they always changed so regularly. No one wanted to put up with Giles's antics for long. They were always happy to take a payoff and run to another firm clutching their non-disclosure agreements and that hard-earned cash." Fiona looked down again.

Callie could hear sirens in the distance, emergency services responding to the calls from the expectant crowd. She had to keep Fiona talking until they got there and could take over.

"Had you planned it all along?"

Fiona looked at her, knowing what she was doing, but still tempted to talk. To explain herself.

"No. I saw the flat up for rent and I thought I would live there and just see if he recognised me. He didn't, of course, didn't even give me a second glance when he passed me in the hallway." She smiled and shook her head. "I still had the keys from when I used to work for him. He'd given me a set so that I could 'drop papers off'. That was always his excuse. What he meant was, so that he could flash you, grope you, pin you to the bed and threaten your career if you dared to complain."

Callie could see tears on her face and feel movement in the crowd behind her, as they were quietly moved back, away from the incident, by the police who had finally arrived.

"I didn't have much of a plan at all, at first. I thought maybe I could do something to hurt him, hurt his career. I used to go into his flat, look around, take things, or move them. My idea was nothing more than to do a bit of gaslighting. Make him think he was going mad by moving things, hiding them, that sort of thing, but then I found his gear, his auto-asphyxiation gear, and the plan, a different plan, began to form. A way to get back at him and all the people who helped him get away with it. You don't think of them, do you?" She challenged Callie.

"The people who facilitate predators like Giles and Adrian? The lawyers who draw up the non-disclosure agreements, the HR bosses who sort out the termination of your employment and the glowing references. The professional associations who turn a blind eye to the complaints because you're just a bit of hysterical totty!"

She almost spat out those words and Callie had to wonder if it was John Dixon or someone else who had used that unfortunate expression.

"Not to mention the colleagues and wives who feign ignorance of just what these men are like."

Callie was at the edge of the rocks now, not quite close enough to reach out and touch Fiona.

"Why don't you come away from the edge?" she said holding out her hand in encouragement.

"And do what?" She looked at Callie intently. "I've spent enough time in institutions thanks to these people. I've no intention of going back to one, to prison." She turned, ready to leap from the edge.

Callie had seen her prepare and launched herself at Fiona, catching her loose clothing and pulling it as hard as she could. The two of them lost balance and crashed on to the ground, just short of the edge. Callie's head hit the hard stone and she was momentarily disorientated, but she could feel people pulling her away, away from Fiona and away from the edge, and then she was in Billy's arms as he helped her to sit up.

"Steady now, you've hurt your head," he said gently as he examined a tender lump on the back of her skull. She could see DS Jeffries crouched next to Fiona, who was lying on her stomach, blood trickling down her face, as he handcuffed her. She looked at Callie with hatred and despair, and Callie wondered if she would ever forgive her for saving her life.

"Ouch!" she said, as Billy touched a particularly tender spot on the back of her head.

"Sorry," he said. "We'd best get you checked out at the hospital; that's quite a lump you've got there."

Callie let Billy fuss as a paramedic came over and examined her. In between having lights shone in her eyes and being asked how she felt for the umpteenth time, she watched as Fiona was formally arrested and led towards a waiting police car. It was only then that DS Jeffries came over to speak to her.

"Nice work, Doc. I would've hated for her to top herself before we managed to arrest her."

"That's a surprise."

He looked at her questioningly.

"I'd have expected you to have been happy to have been saved the bother of a trial and all that," she said gruffly, telling herself that she shouldn't let him get under her skin.

"Yea, but there would still have been loads of paperwork."

She could see from the glint in his eye he wanted to ask her about a lot of things, mostly about finding Miller, but there was no way she wanted to talk about that, so she turned away and allowed Billy and the paramedic to help her up and walk her towards the ambulance.

"Nobody looks at a fat bird twice," Jeffries said to her retreating back. "There's a lesson there somewhere."

Callie gave him a look that she hoped adequately conveyed her feelings at this typically crass remark. He really was the end.

Chapter 32

Billy had insisted on staying the night with Callie once she had been discharged from the emergency department, having been given the all-clear. She was sure she didn't need anyone to keep an eye on her as she hadn't lost consciousness at any point, and apart from a slight headache she had no ill effects. But he said he wanted to be sure she didn't develop any symptoms of concussion and she had to admit that it was nice that someone wanted to make a fuss of her. It was a long time since anyone had cared enough to look after her. She could remember having a bad bout of tonsillitis when she was small and her mother wiping her fevered brow with a handkerchief soaked in cool, fresh Eau de Cologne, and her father smuggling in ice cream to help dull the pain. But she had been a child then and no one had looked after her like that since she had left home.

Callie had a long, relaxing scented bath, as Billy cooked a risotto and fielded phone calls, including from Kate and her mother, both wanting to know what on earth she felt she was doing putting herself in danger by trying to stop a deranged killer from killing herself. Shaky film of the incident, taken by onlookers with their mobile phones, had been shown on the news. Callie knew that most people would think she should have let Fiona jump, but that would have meant too tidy an end.

The world deserved to hear what had turned a beautiful and talented lawyer into a killer; how the system had let her down when she needed its help most. Even if Fiona pled guilty, her lawyer ought to be able to use what had happened to her as mitigating circumstances. And Callie told Billy that she hoped that Fiona herself would understand, in time, how important it was that she tell her story, because time was something she was going to have in abundance. It occurred to Callie that, much as Fiona hadn't wanted to go to prison, she was likely to be looked up to by other prisoners, who might well have been abused by men and let down by lawyers themselves. She might be able to help some of them with appeals and even become something of a hero to them. In time, perhaps Fiona could learn to forgive, if not the men who had abused her, then at least Callie.

As Callie ate her risotto, thinking that Billy was really a surprisingly good cook, certainly much better than she was, she pushed other thoughts to the back of her mind. Tomorrow she would have to think of a way to explain Billy's presence in her flat to her mother, who was probably already checking out mother-of-the-bride outfits online. In fact, she'd actually go and see her parents and let them know that she was fine, but she probably wouldn't subject Billy to meeting them. Not yet. She didn't want to put him off, after all.

Callie was happily dozing next to Billy on the sofa, with the one glass of wine he had allowed her when her doorbell sounded.

"I'll get it." Billy jumped up and went to the intercom.

"Hello?" he said and there was a moment's silence.

"Is Callie in?" Came a disembodied voice that Callie recognised as Miller's. Billy turned to Callie, his eyes silently asking her if she wanted whoever it was to be buzzed in. She nodded, but some of her confusion must have shown on her face, because when he opened the door for Miller, Billy turned to her, said, "I'll just go and get some things out of my car," and tactfully left them.

Miller stood just inside the door and looked as if he had no idea what he ought to do next.

"I'm sorry, I shouldn't have come but I just wanted to thank you," he said and turned to go out again, but Callie stood up and came over to him. He looked terrible. There was a bruise on his cheek and scratches on his neck.

"For goodness sake sit down before you fall down," she told him, and to her relief he did as he was told. "Can I get you anything to drink? Coffee? Brandy?" Callie didn't really think she had any brandy so, goodness knows what she would have done if he had said yes, but he shook his head and sat down heavily.

She sat down next to him and waited for him to tell her what was wrong, although she had a good idea that it was his wife.

After a while, when she was beginning to think she was going to have to prompt him because he was just staring into space and wringing his hands, he said, "She saw the pictures and we had a terrible row." He dropped his head into his hands. "She was screaming at me. I tried to calm her, but…"

Callie could see how much he loved his wife, and how much this must be costing him.

"She kept hitting me and shouting at me and then she ran out of the house and drove away." He sniffed loudly and Callie handed him a tissue from the box on the table in front of them, but he didn't use it.

"Give her time," she said, but he just shook his head.

"I know that Fiona Hutchins had been treated badly. But not by me. And now I've lost my wife."

"I know it's not right, but she believed you hadn't done enough."

"I did everything I could. It wasn't me that was at fault, it was the system."

"I know."

He stood up as they heard Billy coming back up to the flat.

"I'm sorry," Miller said to her and turned, almost barging past Billy in the doorway.

"What was that all about?" Billy asked before correcting himself. "No, no, you don't have to tell me. By the time you get to our age, everyone has a past and I'm not the jealous type."

Callie wondered how she had managed to find such a perfect boyfriend, even though a little tiny part of her had registered the fact that Miller was almost certainly now free and she couldn't deny that her heart beat that little bit faster at the thought.

The End

If you enjoyed this book, please let others know by leaving a quick review on Amazon. Also, if you spot anything untoward in the paperback, get in touch. We strive for the best quality and appreciate reader feedback.

editor@thebookfolks.com

www.thebookfolks.com

ALSO IN THIS SERIES

Available on Kindle and in paperback

DEAD PRETTY – Book 1

When a woman is found dead in Hastings, Sussex, the medical examiner feels a murder has taken place. Yet she feels the police are not doing enough because the victim is a prostitute. Dr Callie Hughes will conduct her own investigation, no matter the danger.

BODY HEAT – Book 2

A series of deadly arson attacks piques the curiosity of Hastings police doctor Callie Hughes. Faced with police incompetence, once again she tries to find the killer herself, but her meddling won't win her any favours and in fact puts her in a compromising position.

VITAL SIGNS – Book 4

When bodies of migrants begin to wash up on the Sussex coast, police doctor Callie Hughes has the unenviable task of inspecting them. But one body stands out to her as different. Convinced that finding the victim's identity will help crack the people smuggling ring, she decides to start her own investigation.

DEADLY REMEDIES – Book 5

When two elderly individuals pass away, it is not an unusual occurrence for seaside town doctor and medical examiner Callie Hughes. But she notices that both of the deceased had a suitcase packed, and her suspicions are aroused. Who is the killer that is prematurely taking them to their final destination?

MURDER LUST – Book 6

After noticing strange marks on the body of a woman found dead in a holiday let, police doctor Callie Hughes probes further. The police take her concerns about a serial killer seriously, but achieve little when another body if found. Callie is possibly the only obstacle to the murderer getting away with the crime, and that makes her a potential target.

OTHER TITLES OF INTEREST

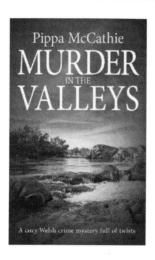

MURDER IN THE VALLEYS by Pippa McCathie

Having left the police following a corruption investigation, ex-superintendent Fabia Havard is struggling with civilian life. When a girl is murdered in her town, she can't help trying to find the killer. Will her former colleague Matt Lambert stop her, or realize the value of his former boss to the floundering inquiry?

Available in paperback, audio and on Kindle

THE WOMAN BEHIND HER by Anna Willett

When Jackie Winter inherits her aunt's house, she makes a
chilling discovery. Worse, she finds that she is being
watched. When someone is murdered nearby, she finds
herself in the frame. Can she join up the dots and prove
her innocence?

Available on Kindle and in paperback.

Printed in Great Britain
by Amazon

28149353R00146